AMATEUR HOUR

A Novel of Suspense

by Robert Hardin

The Bobbs-Merrill Company, Inc.
Indianapolis / New York

Library of Congress Cataloging in Publication Data

Hardin, Robert.
   Amateur hour.

   I. Title.
PZ4.H26227Am   [PS3558.A62317]   813'.5'4   76-46699
ISBN 0-672-52255-1

AMATEUR HOUR

1

It was twelve noon on a spring day in San Francisco, and in a few minutes, after years of drastically informal education, I would be a lawyer. I waited with the other applicants for the current president of the Bar Association to swear us in. My wife, Jennifer, and her father, Abe, were in the audience.

"David Armstrong."

I shook the man's hand, grabbed the piece of paper, and hurried off the stage toward Jennifer's beckoning face. She was twenty-eight, but when she wore her freshly washed long dark hair straight down around her ears, as she did today, she looked closer to eighteen. I embraced her and Abe in turn, and then the three of us got into the car for the return to Sausalito.

As the car headed toward the Golden Gate Bridge, I was uncharacteristically quiet, reflecting not so much on the struggle that was behind me as on the uncertainty that lay ahead. A lot of people were getting law degrees and embarking on new careers, but not too many of them were forty years of age, as I was, with the desire to be the Clarence Darrow of their day. I took the first exit after the bridge, following the twisting road down the hill toward our apartment.

"Have you quit your job already, David?" Abe asked.

"Yes. Jennifer and I have enough money to last us about six months," I said. "Then we'll have to see. I can always get another sales job, though."

As we entered our apartment I noticed a wooden shingle hanging over the door to the guest bedroom, which I used as an office.

DAVID ARMSTRONG
Attorney at Law

We all admired Jennifer's handiwork, then gravitated toward the terrace overlooking the bay. Jennifer brought out wine and snacks. I turned on the radio, and Abe and I relaxed in the afternoon sun, watching the sailboats crisscross our horizon. I didn't know it then, but it was to be one of the last peaceful moments I would have for several weeks.

Seven years before, I had maneuvered myself into a bad job and a bad marriage in New York. After divorcing both the wife and the job, I married Jennifer and came to San Francisco. Thinking I had put all my troubles behind me, I was ready for a new life. But it didn't happen quite that easily, and had it not been for Abe, I probably would have again descended to the same state of frustration I'd reached in New York.

Abe had himself come to the Bay Area a few years

2

before us, after his own divorce. He owned a seaside garage and home in Bodega Bay, about fifty miles up the coast, and in his spare time he was a lay analyst. Neither Jennifer nor I had initially been inclined toward his theories, which were principally Adlerian, but the force of Abe's mind and personality had eventually persuaded us. His philosophy was now a major influence in our lives, and I had come to love him as much as Jennifer did.

"Abe," I said suddenly, as if he knew what I had been thinking, "you know this day would never have been possible without you."

He smiled at me and then at Jennifer, who had joined us with a tray of cheese, crackers and wine-filled glasses.

"You two did all the work," he said. "I was merely the foreman leaning on the shovel." He raised his glass and added, "But today's your day, David. Congratulations."

We all clinked our glasses together and tasted the wine.

"Now, how do you get some clients?" Abe asked. "Where does a new attorney find customers?"

I hesitated before answering, wondering whether to spring my surprise yet; but Jennifer spoke up: "He won't have any trouble finding the kind he's looking for."

"I see you two still have a basic philosophical dispute," Abe said.

"On that subject we do," Jennifer agreed. "And now that David's really a lawyer, it's no longer just a discussion. He doesn't want to defend mere criminals. He wants to defend the very worst, the most despicable."

"But that's the whole point," I said. "A criminal attorney can no more refuse to defend a client than a doctor can decide not to treat a sick patient."

"That's an illogical comparison, David," Jennifer said. "Doctors do have to treat patients, but they don't necessarily want to handle the worst cases."

"Okay, but the point I'm trying to make is that a person arrested by the police is in big trouble; with the exception of a serious illness, the biggest trouble of his life. And just as a doctor would not deny aid to a sick man, no matter what the man had done, I'll use my professional skills to help anyone. You think it's *because* of the crime they're accused of that I want to defend them, but that's not true. I want to defend them *in spite* of the crime they're accused of."

"I'm sorry I brought it up," Jennifer said. "It's the same old argument, and you know how I feel. No matter what you say, if I were a criminal attorney, there are some people I simply could not defend."

"But they're not guilty just because you read about them in the newspaper. One day a guy is a husband, a father, a factory worker; and the next, before any kind of trial, he's a robber or a murderer, with all the power of the state stacked against him. They say 'the People versus the Defendant,' and they mean it. Everybody in the whole state against this one citizen. Everybody, that is, except me."

Jennifer held up her hands, surrendering the point, but I was caught up in my own argument.

"The law-and-order types are always yelling because judges turn criminals loose, but they don't realize that there is no such thing as an automatic appeal. The only time any case can be reversed is when the lower court has violated some fundamental right of the accused. If, instead of trying to bulldoze people into jails, the police would simply give them fair trials, they would have their law and order. But they don't do it, because they have

4

no faith in their own system. The police, of all people, really don't understand the whole thing. They say they have a tough job, and they're right, but that's the way it should be in our society. The only place where police have an easy time is in a police state, which is why I'll use all my energies to see that anyone—and I mean anyone—can get a fair trial."

Abe and Jennifer broke into mock applause.

I bowed and grinned, saying, "I'm sorry about the outburst, but you both know how I feel." I glanced at my watch. "It's almost time for the news. Let's watch it. I've got a surprise for you."

We situated ourselves in the living room, and after a few more minutes of music the hourly news broadcast came on. There were some national stories, and then:

Another development in the Bay Ripper case was announced by the mayor today when he revealed that there are now rewards totaling over one hundred thousand dollars for any information leading to the capture and conviction of the man or men responsible for these killings. The twenty-four-hour number to call is 877-7777, and the mayor assured complete confidentiality to anyone telephoning. He also took the opportunity to warn all women, but especially women living alone, to be extremely cautious about allowing strange men into their apartments under any circumstances. The police have found no evidence of forced entry in any of the seven murders to date. These seven women have all been sexually assaulted and killed in San Francisco in the past few months by a man authorities call the Bay Ripper because the savage mutilation of the victims' bodies resembles the infamous Jack the Ripper case in England a cen-

5

tury ago. Again, the number to call is 877-7777.

In other crime news, a city health department orderly assigned to the Hall of Justice Rape Bureau has himself been charged with rape. Ralph Rodriguez of 1031 Mission Street was arrested yesterday after a rape victim in the office for an examination identified him as the man who had raped her in her Telegraph Hill apartment the night before. Police are withholding the identity of the young woman for the time being for her own safety, but it is known that she is the heiress to a large midwestern fortune. Rodriguez is to be arraigned tomorrow morning.

I switched off the radio and leaned back against a beanbag.

"I'm going to defend that man," I stated.

"Rodriguez? How do you know?" Jennifer asked.

"I heard the report earlier this morning before meeting you two downtown. I went to his home and spoke to his wife and his mother. They hadn't gotten a lawyer yet, so I offered them my services. I told them I was new but free. They agreed, and I'm the attorney of record for tomorrow's hearing."

Abe waved his wineglass at me and said, "Good luck on your first case, David."

Jennifer frowned and looked at me for what seemed like a long time before saying, "A rapist."

"An accused rapist," I corrected, and her face relaxed into a smile.

She joined me on the floor. "I'm really happy for you, David. No matter what I said, I think it's great."

I kissed her and beamed at Abe. "I think it's great too. In fact, I can't wait for tomorrow morning."

2

The next morning at ten o'clock I walked into the Hall of Justice for the first time as a lawyer. During the past few years I had spent countless afternoons here, unknown to my sales manager, watching criminal lawyers at work. I knew that California was no more effective than other states in locking up its troublemakers, but the courts maintained at least an appearance of justice and fairness. My only other experience with courtrooms had been in New York, with its loud slaughterhouse atmosphere, and while I realized that San Francisco's several hundred thousand people were far easier to manage than New York's millions, I was always impressed by the quiet and unhurried pace of the Hall of Justice. Today, however, I was as frightened by it as if I were on trial myself. I had done a lot of things in my life, but I had never before been directly responsible for another human being's freedom. As I took the elevator up to the second floor, I told myself that even though I lacked experience, no lawyer on earth would devote more time and energy than I would to my first case.

Rodriguez's wife and his mother were waiting for me outside the courtroom. Both were dressed almost totally in black, as if they were going to a funeral.

"Is my son all right?" his mother asked. "Have you seen him?"

"No, I telephoned him last night and told him I would speak to him today, before court. He seemed all right. He asked me to bring him some cigarettes." I pointed to the bulge in my briefcase to indicate the carton I had brought.

"Good," his mother said. "We went to the bail man, like you told us."

She handed me the bail contract. I had never seen one before. It looked like an insurance policy.

"That's fine," I assured her, returning the papers to her. "As soon as your son's case is over, you call the bail man, and he'll get Ralph out for you."

She nodded her understanding. She was less than five feet tall, and I felt like a giant standing over her. Rodriguez's wife was not much taller, and although she was obviously years younger than his mother, both of them had lost all vestiges of youth. I guided them into the courtroom and, after seating them in the spectator area, walked up to the clerk of the court, requesting a copy of the complaint against Ralph Rodriguez. He flipped through the papers on his desk and handed me some yellow pages along with a blank to fill out. After

8

writing in my name and address, I handed it back to him and asked to have my client brought up for an interview.

While waiting, I joined the two Rodriguez women and watched the arraignment parade. A young housewife from the Richmond district got a ten-dollar fine for permitting her dog to run unleashed, and a nineteen-year-old prostitute pleaded guilty to her first offense. The judge spoke to her but stared past her into the courtroom at her pimp. In the midst of this, a sheriff's deputy motioned for me to follow him into a room behind the court where a large caged elevator brought prisoners up from the jail. The deputy opened the cage door and a tall, muscular Mexican dressed in hospital whites stepped out. The deputy directed us to a small interview room nearby and waited outside.

"I'm Dave Armstrong," I said, offering my hand.

Rodriguez shook it and said, "I appreciate your coming here, mister, but, like I told you on the phone, we don't have any money."

I took the carton of cigarettes out of my briefcase and threw them on the table. Rodriguez sat down and tore out a pack. I took out my pipe and tobacco, then lit his cigarette with my lighter.

"As I told your wife and your mother, I don't want any money," I said. "I'm a new lawyer. This is my first case. I'm willing to take it for the experience."

Rodriguez jumped up. "I'm no guinea pig, man. I want a real lawyer."

The deputy peeked in, but I waved him away. "Look," I said, pulling Rodriguez back down into his chair, "if you can't afford a lawyer, they'll assign a public defender to you. Those guys have to worry about fifty cases at a time. You're the only client I've got. Take your choice."

Rodriguez looked at me for some time, smoking his cigarette with extreme pleasure. Finally he asked, "You any good?"

I replied by waving the complaint at him. "We'll find out soon enough. They're going to call our case any minute, so let's get busy."

After getting the biographical data on my note-pad—*Ralph Rodriguez, age twenty-nine. Wife, Anna, age twenty-five. Four children. Mother and younger sister also living with him*—I probed further. His father, dead now, had worked as a janitor for the public schools all his life and had formed his own business cleaning service a few years before his death. Ralph had followed him into city civil service, passing the examination after graduation from Mission High School. He had taken a job with the Health Department and had worked as an orderly at San Francisco General Hospital for several years. Five months earlier, he had been assigned as a technical assistant to the doctor in charge of the Rape Bureau at the Hall of Justice. To support his family, he had tried to keep the cleaning business going during his off hours.

"Okay," I said, "now tell me about this girl. I want to know everything that happened. And I want to know the truth, no matter what it is. It won't have any effect on what I do in court, because my job is to defend you to the best of my ability, and that's what I plan to do. And everything you tell me is strictly between us. Under-stand? Also, I think I have some idea of how you feel, since several years ago I sat where you're sitting myself. I would have gone to jail if a good lawyer hadn't saved

10

my tail." I paused, then added, "So, where were you the night this girl was raped?"

"I was cleaning up a restaurant. One of my clients."

"Which one and where?"

"The Old Mexico on Twenty-fourth and Protero."

I wrote it down. "From what time to what time?"

"I got home from work about six, had dinner, watched TV until about ten, then took the cleaning van to the restaurant. I was back home by one in the morning."

I wrote it down without reacting, but it didn't sound good. "And you were in the Old Mexico all that time?"

"Yeah."

"Anybody with you? Did anybody see you?"

He shook his head. "No. I have my own key. They close at ten. I go there after everybody leaves and clean up."

Without pausing after his answer, I quickly asked, "Did you rape her, Ralph?"

"No, man. What are you, the D.A.?"

I leaned back and relit my pipe. "I'm just making sure I get the story straight. Tell me what happened when they arrested you. What they said to you. What you said to them. Everything. Okay?"

Rodriguez talked for the next several minutes without interruption. When he had finished, I said, "If you're telling me the truth, we've got a chance, Ralph. It's a small one, but it's a chance. I'll have to do some checking, but the way you were identified by that girl sounds shaky. I may be able to get it thrown out. If that's all they've got, we'll win. But we won't know all their ammunition until the preliminary hearing. Today is just arraignment and bail. Your wife and your mother

11

gave the deed to your house to a bail bondsman, and everything is set up. You'll be out an hour after your case is heard. Any questions?"

"No, sir."

"All right, let's relax a minute then and wait for the call." I lit another cigarette for him and then looked over my notes. I was still anxious, but I was also impatient to get going. I had a wild idea that required research to see if it was at all legally possible. And I wanted to check on the girl. Her name was not revealed in the complaint, but Ralph had heard them call her Wendy Horn. She was the heiress to the Horn Baking Company fortune in Minneapolis. I had read about her in the society columns.

The deputy told us the case was called, and we entered the courtroom.

"Is Ralph Rodriguez your name?" the clerk droned.

"Yes," Ralph responded.

"Is your attorney present in court?"

Rodriguez said yes again, and the clerk handed the papers to the judge.

"Your honor," I said, "my name is David Armstrong, and I have filed a Notice of Appearance with the court."

The judge glanced over the complaint and asked me whether I waived the reading of it.

"Yes, your honor, we waive the reading for the record, and the defendant is ready for a preliminary hearing. Before bail is set, I would like to state that Mr. Rodriguez is a native of San Francisco and has lived at his present address for over twenty years. He is married; he has four children and a mother and sister living with him for whom he is the sole support. He has worked for the city for eleven years and has never before been arrested or charged with any crime. Because of the nature of the charges, we understand that releasing the defendant on his own recognizance may not be possible, but we do request a reasonable bail so that he may continue to support his family during the proceedings."

I had not paused for breath during my speech, which sounded to me as if it had been delivered in another man's voice. My legs were twitching. I clasped my left hand over Ralph's clenched right fist, partly to reassure him and partly to conceal my own nervousness.

The judge asked the Assistant District Attorney for comment, but he had none.

"Bail is set at five thousand dollars," the judge said without hesitation. "Let's schedule a hearing for the day after tomorrow, if that's convenient for you, Mr. Armstrong?"

I took my appointment book out of my suit pocket and looked at the blank pages. "The eighteenth is fine, your honor."

"The eighteenth, then, at ten o'clock."

The deputy led Ralph out of the courtroom, and I went back to his wife and his mother. After they called the bail bondsman, I told them where to wait for Ralph's release, then left. I knew they would have preferred for me to stay with them, but I wanted to be alone for a while to think and to calm down.

As I walked down the steps onto Bryant Street, I saw the nineteen-year-old prostitute getting into her pimp's Cadillac and thought how fast she had made bail. I hoped Ralph's bondsman was that good. When I crossed the street to my car, I saw a ticket on the windshield.

It had been my first day as a lawyer. Between the ticket and the cigarettes I had bought, it had cost me fifteen dollars. And I had yet to make my first dime.

3

Jennifer taught ballet and tap dancing at a private school in the Sunset district. Since I did not have to pick her up for a couple of hours, I left the ticket on the windshield of the car and went into a bar for a beer and a sandwich.

While sipping the beer and waiting for the sandwich, I reviewed the notes I had taken and planned my next steps. First thing tomorrow I would type out a subpoena for the police records of the case and get the judge to sign it. That would enable me to verify Rodriguez's version of the arrest and identification procedures. Then I would pay a visit to the Assistant District Attorney in charge of the case. Between what he might tell me and the police records, I would know how to pro-

15

ceed the following day at the preliminary hearing.

After eating a terrible tuna fish sandwich and drowning it with a second beer, I got into my car and drove up California Street, cut through the park, and waited for Jennifer. It was still over an hour before she got off work, so I turned on an afternoon talk show on the radio, pushed my seat into a reclining position, and listened to my neighbors call in and argue about the day's events. By the time Jennifer came out I was completely relaxed, the tension of the morning forgotten.

Jennifer was still dressed in a leotard, her hair rolled up in a bun. I kissed her wet face, and as I started the car she immediately began telling me about her day, as she always did, about this kid and that one; and then she caught herself.

"I'm sorry, David," she said. "Habit. How was *your* day? Your first day?"

"Fantastic," I replied. "I was a little nervous at first, but I loved every minute of it. And I may have a chance to get the guy off."

"How?"

"Well, he works as an assistant to the doctor at the Rape Bureau in the Hall of Justice," I explained. "The girl who was raped came into the Bureau for an examination the morning after the crime and when she saw Rodriguez she told the doctor he was the man who had raped her. The doctor went upstairs and got the cops, and they took him into custody, interrogated him, then showed him to the girl through a one-way mirror. According to the complaint, she positively identified him."

"What's wrong with that?" Jennifer wondered.

16

"A lot, I think. It was dark when she was attacked, and she couldn't have gotten a very good look. Her description could fit any Chicano in the city. And the very first Chicano she sees the next day, she says is the guy who did it. For all I know, all Chicanos look alike to her. I just don't like the way it sounds. But in any case the police should have made sure a lawyer was present before they confronted him with an accuser, or at least tested her by making her choose him out of a lineup."

"Sounds technical to me. Do you think he raped her?"

"I really don't know, Jennifer. But I do know that if that's the basis of their evidence against him, they've got a weak case."

"Where are we going?" Jennifer asked suddenly, noticing that I was not taking the usual route home.

"Greenwich Street," I said. "We're paying a call on a member of the Now Society."

"The girl who was raped?"

I nodded. "Rodriguez heard her name. She's Wendy Horn, of *the* Horns. There's a W. Horn on Greenwich. I'm sure she's the one."

"Oh, David, are you sure it's all right? Are you allowed to talk to her?"

"Of course. She doesn't have to speak with me if she doesn't want to, but I have a perfect right to interview her on behalf of my client, and I plan to do just that."

Our small car strained up the last, steepest grade of Greenwich Street. The hill finally leveled off and we were overlooking the waterfront. I pulled over to the curb.

"Come with me," I said to Jennifer. "If she happens

17

to say anything I can use, I'll need you as a third-party witness."

The house was a two-story apartment building on the edge of the cliff. On one of the mailboxes I read "Horn, W. and Pell, A." I wondered whether she lived with another girl or a man. When I started to ring the bell I heard a nervous voice behind me.

"Freeze. Don't move a muscle." Then, coming closer, the voice said, "Both of you lean forward. Put your hands over your heads and up against the wall. Now. Move."

We complied with the instructions, and then I felt the cold tip of a gun barrel behind my left ear. A hand patted the length of my body, then removed my billfold. Jennifer was undergoing a similar search next to me.

"All right," the voice said, "you can drop your hands and turn around, but slow, and tell us what you're doing here."

We turned around to see two men in business suits facing us. Both of them were still holding their revolvers on us.

"I'm a lawyer," I said evenly, "and if you two are policemen, you'd better identify yourselves before we go any further."

The larger of the two men took a step toward us, and when he spoke I realized that he had been the one who had done the talking.

"Mister, the only identifying going on around here will be yours. There's a goddamned mass murderer running around loose, and you show up at a rape victim's house when we haven't released her name to the

18

public. Now, I'm asking you one last time—what in the hell are you doing here? How did you find her?"

"I'm the defense counsel in this case," I said quickly. "My client overheard her name, and I came here to interview her."

The man shook his head. "Can you prove that?"

"Yes, we can," Jennifer said—to my surprise, for I had no credentials to indicate my new profession; I hadn't even ordered business cards yet. Jennifer reached in her purse and produced the certificate I had been given by the Bar Association at yesterday's ceremony.

The man glanced at it, then handed it to the other man. "A new one," he said. "The ink's barely dry. Watch them a minute."

"I was going to get it framed," Jennifer whispered to me as the man walked over to an unmarked automobile and exchanged conversation with someone on the radio.

When he returned, he said, "Okay, you can go."

I hesitated, but the man slapped my billfold into my chest and gave me a firm push. "You can speak to Miss Horn in court, counselor."

I glanced at Jennifer, and we silently agreed to retreat. Neither of us spoke until we were across the bridge and almost home. Then Jennifer broke the silence.

"San Francisco police, one; new attorney and wife, nothing."

We both laughed far beyond the humor of the joke, and I said, "We're lucky you had the certificate." I stopped the car in front of our apartment building and told Jennifer to go on in and shower; I would pick up a pizza in town.

When I returned we ate the pizza on the floor in front of the fireplace, sipped red wine and watched the moon rays reflected in the bay water.

The phone rang. It was Abe calling from Bodega Bay.

"Dad wants to know how your first day in court went," Jennifer yelled across the room.

"Just tell him the score—one to nothing," I shouted back.

4

The morning came in with a thick fog and cold rain. I perked the coffee while I showered, then dressed, found some classical music on the stereo, and, despite the chill, drank my liquid breakfast on the terrace. A brown pelican was teaching a flock of smaller pelicans how to spear for fish, and gulls were circling in the rain trying to coax me into feeding them, but my thoughts were across the bay in the Hall of Justice. I was a lawyer defending a client against criminal charges, and although this fulfilled a lifelong dream, I was still a little anxious about the whole thing.

I went into the bedroom and pulled the covers up around Jennifer's neck. I whispered that I had set the alarm in time for her bus, but she did not stir. She loved her sleep. I kissed her softly on the cheek and left.

21

When I got downtown, I parked the car two blocks from Bryant Street, deciding not to risk another ticket.

I passed through the weapons detector at the entrance to the Hall of Justice and paused in front of the directory sign. The Inspectors Bureau was on the fourth floor; the Rape Bureau was on the main floor, Room 100. I followed the numbers down the long hallway until I came to the last office, which had a glass front and a glass door. Two women were seated at a table equipped with half a dozen telephones.

"Could I speak to Ralph Rodriguez?" I asked as I walked in, although I knew he did not plan to go back to work until his trial was over.

"He's not here, sir," the woman nearest me said, getting up. "May I help you?"

"No, I'm just a friend," I explained. Looking around, I saw that the right side of the office was furnished like a doctor's waiting room, with a couch, chairs, and a table with magazines; the side where the two women were seated was equipped with desks, telephones, tape recorders, typewriters, and a large coffee pot. Near the door stood a pamphlet rack offering governmental publications about rape. There was another door at the rear of the office, which I surmised to be the examining room, but the glass was opaque. I thought better of interviewing Ralph's boss just yet, so I backed out the front door.

I took the elevator to the second floor and the same courtroom where I had appeared yesterday. The doors were still closed, and several people were waiting in the hallway. I found a small door around the corner which led to the judge's chambers, and the bailiff allowed me entrance after I showed him my subpoena. I caught a

22

glimpse of the judge in his room, seated behind his modern desk, surrounded by law books, still not wearing a robe, drinking coffee. He signed the proffered paper without a question, and the bailiff brought it back to me. I had carefully typed the subpoena last night, copying the words from a form book, doing it over several times until I had it exactly right, but now for the first time it seemed real to me. The judge's signature ordered the police to give me any and all records relating to Ralph's arrest no later than ten tomorrow morning, the time and date of the hearing.

With the freshly authenticated document in my hand, I rode the elevator up two more floors to the Inspectors Bureau. A uniformed policeman occupied the reception desk. Behind him was a regiment of desks, occasionally broken by a glass-walled cubicle. I asked to speak to the arresting officer in the Rodriguez case. The policeman excused himself, then returned and escorted me through the large room until we came to an office in the rear. The sign on the door read CHIEF OF INSPECTORS.

I introduced myself to the man inside the office, who motioned me to a chair facing his desk and said, "I'm Inspector Casey, Mr. Armstrong. What can I do for you?"

"I don't know, Inspector. I just wanted to serve the arresting officer of Ralph Rodriguez with a subpoena. An Inspector Hansen, I believe? I'm the counsel in the case."

Casey nodded. "I see. Well, Inspector Hansen reports to me. You can leave it here."

I handed him the subpoena as he stood up. He was dressed in a bright blue suit with a red tie and was a lot

23

younger than I would have expected a man in his position to be. He walked me back to the elevator. Just as the doors opened, he said, "See you in court, Mr. Armstrong, and, by the way, I hear the view from Telegraph Hill last night was breathtaking. Did you happen to catch it?"

The doors closed before I could answer, and I could hear his laughter most of the way back down to the lobby. Casey had flustered me so much that I neglected to push the button for the third-floor offices of the District Attorney, so I waited for the elevator to refill and rode it back up.

A woman receptionist asked me to sign the visitors' register in the District Attorney's office and promised to find out which of the staff was assigned to my case. Eventually, a young man of no more than thirty came out to meet me. He was dressed in a striped and vested suit and wore tortoiseshell glasses.

"Bud Randall's my name," he said. "I understand you're defending Mr. Rodriguez. Let's go into my office."

His "office" was really only a stall. There must have been sixty small rooms on either side of a long hallway, and none of them had doors. It reminded me of a Chinese restaurant with booths.

After we had situated ourselves at his desk, Randall asked, "Do you normally try criminal cases, Mr. Armstrong? I don't recall seeing you around the courts before."

"I don't normally try any kind of cases," I replied. "I'm a brand-new lawyer. This is my first case."

Randall tried unsuccessfully to conceal his surprise at this information, in view of my age; then he said, "I see.

24

Welcome to the profession. Where did you go to law school?"

"I didn't," I confessed. "I never went to law school." When Randall did not respond, I added, "I took a correspondence course."

"You're kidding," he suggested.

"No, I'm not. Aren't you aware that California is the one state in the union where you can still do that?"

He shook his head. "No. You mean that's all you did? You've never apprenticed with anyone, never been in court?"

I laughed and said, "No. I just read the law books, but I passed the same bar exam you did."

Randall seemed flabbergasted. He leaned back in his chair and stared at me for a moment. Finally he shook his head again and said, "I really don't know whether to believe you or not, Mr. Armstrong, but it doesn't matter. If you're here to plea-bargain for Rodriguez, I'm afraid I can't help you at all. We've decided to go all the way with this one."

"No, I didn't come here to plea-bargain," I said. "I came here to discuss the evidence with you. I've subpoenaed the police records for the hearing tomorrow, so I don't know for sure yet, but from what my client tells me, it looks pretty weak."

"In what way?"

"Well, the way the police had the girl identify him. I think it was improper procedure."

"Then contest it at a *Wade* hearing, but you should know, if you got as far as the Ks in correspondence school, that *Kirby v. Illinois* is the guideline now.

I did not reply to the sarcasm, and Randall quickly added, "I'm sorry, Armstrong; that was uncalled for.

But I'm not going to help you with your case. Rape prosecutions are very difficult, but we've got a spontaneous identification by the victim in this one, and we think we can make it stick."

He stood up and offered me his hand. "I'm afraid that's all I can tell you today."

I shook his hand and walked out—with nothing. It was raining hard now, but I decided to walk anyway. I had gained nothing from my encounters with Randall and Casey, but I had gotten a feel for my opposition. There was still some anxiety inside me, but with renewed energy I found myself practically racing up the steps of City Hall toward the law library.

After nearly three hours of research, I had what I needed—a plan. Unless there was something Rodriguez had not told me about the way he had been arrested and identified, the precedents supported me. Even *Kirby*. I returned all the books to the shelves, packed up my notes, thanked the librarian, and walked back to my car. There was still time to see Ralph and prepare for tomorrow.

I worked my way through the confusing angle of downtown streets until I found Mission Street. I parked in front of his house. A low-level fence with a gate surrounded a small yard, and a van sat in the driveway. The faded letters on the side of the van read AAA MAINTENANCE. A small child answered my knock, then ran into the kitchen yelling something in Spanish. Ralph's mother came, wiping her hands on her apron and smoothing her dress; and invited me into the living room.

"My son is coming now," she said. "I make him rest today."

She directed me to a couch covered with a cotton

26

blanket. The television set was on, and I could smell pungent odors from the kitchen. A crucifix hung on the wall facing me, and there was a black-velvet portrait of Jesus over a doorway. The children peeked out at me from the hall entrance, as did Ralph's wife, who, I realized, had never spoken a single word to me.

"Does Ralph have a suit to wear in court?" I asked his mother.

"Yes, sir. The one he was married in. A blue one. I press it for him."

Ralph came into the room, pulling on a shirt, and sat down across from me. By the time he had lit a cigarette his mother had gone into the kitchen and returned with a cup of black coffee for him. She offered me one also, but I declined.

"I celebrated pretty good last night," Ralph said.

I nodded and asked him whether he had any friends who were about the same build as he. "Mexicans?"

"Chicanos," he corrected.

I nodded my assent, and he replied, "Sure. Why?"

"I want you to have them in court with you tomorrow morning, as many of them as you can get. A dozen, if possible, but at least six or seven. And have them dress in blue suits if they have them. Do you think you can do that? It's very important."

"Yeah, I think so. A couple of guys were coming anyway. What's going on?"

"That girl says she was raped in the dark, so I don't know how she could get a good look at her attacker. I doubt very seriously if she could pick you out of a group of men, especially a group of Chicanos."

"Wow," Rodriguez said. "Will they allow you to do that?"

"We won't know for sure until tomorrow, but right

27

now you've got to get busy and round up all the guys you can."

Rodriguez hopped up. "Man, if this works, I'll be cleared. Right?"

"Right," I agreed, but cautioned, "If this works."

5

Since Friday was Jennifer's day off, she accompanied me to the Hall of Justice; we planned to go to Bodega Bay after the hearing to spend the weekend with Abe. Although we arrived at the courtroom early, Ralph and his wife and mother and five friends were already seated in the rear of the room—on the very last row, as if they were afraid to penetrate any further into an unknown environment. I was pleased to see that two of the men were wearing similar blue suits and that one of them resembled Ralph enough to have been his brother.

Jennifer and I slid into the row ahead of the group and introduced ourselves. Another hearing was in progress, which prevented us from talking, so I faced the bench and studied the judge, a heavyset man with a full red beard much like my own. The back doors swung open and Randall came in, followed by Inspector Casey and another man whom I did not recognize. They seated themselves on the front row.

When Inspector Casey got up and took some papers to the court clerk, I followed him to the desk, and we nodded to each other in passing. I identified myself to the clerk and he gave me the police records I had subpoenaed. Back in my seat, I flipped through the file while I waited for Ralph's name to be called.

"Look at this," I whispered to Jennifer. "It's even better than I thought. She even said the rapist had a moustache."

Before Jennifer had a chance to respond, the case was called. Jennifer squeezed my hand and wished me good luck. Ralph and I took our places at the defense table.

The judge asked whether the parties were ready to proceed. When both Randall and I stated our readiness, he said, "Very well. If there are any witnesses in the court, you are instructed to wait outside until you are called."

Randall spoke up. "Your honor, our first witness, Inspector Hansen, is present in court. We'd like to call him now."

So Hansen was the other man I had seen come in with Randall and Casey. Wearing a plain gray suit, he was tall and sturdily built, tough looking. Unlike Casey's, his appearance was not misleading. He had been a cop for a long time, and he looked it.

Randall led him routinely through the circumstances of Rodriguez's arrest: names, dates, hours. When it was my turn to question him, I waved him off the stand without a word. Randall's next witness was Doctor Charlotte Paley.

Doctor Paley was a large woman, probably between fifty and fifty-five, not fat but squarely built and almost six feet tall. She had tinted red hair and the coldest blue-gray eyes I had ever seen. She was wearing a white lab coat over a skirt and a cashmere sweater.

She testified that she had worked as a physician in the city's Health Department for thirty-two years. At the beginning of this year she had been assigned to the newly created Rape Bureau at the Hall of Justice. She said she believed this had come about because so many rape victims had complained of having to go to the Central Emergency Hospital to be examined by male doctors. Because of the nature of her duties, she was on call around the clock and responded to an electronic beeper whenever she was needed.

According to her testimony, she had gone to Wendy Horn's apartment less than an hour after the rape was first reported, about two in the morning, she believed; she had taken a vaginal smear and blood sample and had examined Miss Horn thoroughly. She had also given her a shot of penicillin in case of VD. She said Miss Horn refused a sedative, and she instructed her to come to the office the next day for the results of the blood test, which would determine whether further treatment would be necessary.

"That would have been a Sunday?" Randall suggested, and when she agreed, he asked, "Did she come to your office the next day?"

"Yes, sir. I informed her that there was no trace of disease and no chance of conception, since she was already taking an oral preventative."

"And what happened, if anything, after that, Doctor?"

Doctor Paley glanced over at Rodriguez before an-

31

swering. "Well, as Miss Horn was leaving, she turned back and asked me who the man was in my outer office. I told her he was our medical technician, Mr. Rodriguez, and she told me . . ."

"Just a moment, Doctor," Randall interrupted. "If you recognize Mr. Rodriguez in the courtroom, would you please point him out?"

"He's sitting right there," she said, pointing to Ralph in the seat next to me.

"Let the record indicate that the witness identified the defendant Rodriguez," Randall said to the court clerk. Then he asked Doctor Paley if it was not unusual for Ralph to have been working on a Sunday.

"No, sir. We always work on the weekends and take weekdays off. There is a much greater incidence of rape on Saturday and Sunday."

"Very well. What happened next?"

"Miss Horn told me she thought Mr. Rodriguez looked like the man who had raped her."

"And what did you do then?"

"I asked one of the volunteer women in the office to sit with her while I went next door to the precinct and told them what had happened. Inspector Hansen arrived shortly afterwards and took Mr. Rodriguez and Miss Horn away."

"Thank you very much, Doctor Paley," Randall said. Then he turned to me. "Your witness, counselor."

I stood up, holding the police report in my hand, and said, "Just one question, Doctor. Do you recall Miss Horn's exact words when she told you she thought she recognized Mr. Rodriguez?"

She hesitated. "Exactly?"

"Well, did she say 'That's the man,' or 'I think he's the

man,' or 'I think he might look like the man,' or what?"

Doctor Paley paused, then said, "To the best of my memory, she said, 'I think he looks like the man who raped me.' "

"And have you ever seen Mr. Rodriguez wear a moustache?"

"No, I have not."

I excused her from the witness stand and sat down. My legs had been trembling, but I felt good. The trap had been set, and now it was time for the bait. Randall called Wendy Horn to the stand. As the bailiff went to escort her into court, I reached into my briefcase and took out the brown paper bag I had prepared the night before. I had cut out two eye holes and a mouth, turning it into a makeshift mask.

"Put this over your head as soon as she comes in," I whispered to Ralph.

He looked at me quizzically but accepted the bag under the table.

When Wendy Horn followed the bailiff into the courtroom, there was a murmur from the crowd. Along with everyone else, I had been anticipating the appearance of the mystery victim, but I was not prepared for one of the most beautiful women I had ever seen. Tall, long-limbed, and very curvaceous, she was also unabashedly sexual. The simple and demure dress she had chosen for her court appearance did not conceal the sensuousness it barely contained. Neither the judge nor anyone else noticed the bag over Ralph's head until Wendy Horn had situated herself on the witness stand.

Then, "What is the meaning of this, Mr. Armstrong?" the judge suddenly demanded.

I rose. "Your honor, the defense contends that this

witness's identification of the accused was tainted by improper pretrial procedures, and we object to any in-court identification until this has been ruled on."

Randall jumped to his feet. "Your honor, this is highly irregular, and we strenuously protest."

The judge glared at me for a moment, then turned solicitously to Wendy Horn.

"Miss Horn, would you please wait outside again for a few minutes while we clear this up?" He banged his gavel and announced a fifteen-minute recess. "I'll see counsel in my chambers."

I told Ralph to take the bag off and rejoin his family. I picked up my briefcase and followed Randall into the judge's office behind the courtroom.

The judge motioned us into the leather chairs facing him. Randall was furious.

"Of all the . . ."

The judge held up his hand, silencing Randall. "That was a cheap trick, Mr. Armstrong," he said, lighting a cigarette. "You're very close to contempt. What did you hope to achieve?"

To conceal my nervousness, I filled my pipe. "Your honor, as I stated in court, I think the whole pretrial procedure here violated due process."

Randall said, "Judge, we had a spontaneous ID by the girl in the doctor's office and a separate, positive ID in the police station. Besides, if Armstrong objects to that evidence, he'll have to do it at a separate hearing. All we're required to do today is to show cause to hold the defendant for trial." He seemed baffled that there could be any question about it.

I lighted my pipe and said, "I'm well aware of the defense's right to a separate hearing under *Wade*

34

guidelines. However, in this case, the only evidence linking the accused to the crime is the victim's identification of him. If we can show that identification to be improper or unsure, I believe the best place for dismissal is at this hearing. It would save time and money, and I can cite several cases where such dismissals have taken place at preliminary hearings."

"Are you making a motion to suppress, then?" the judge asked.

"No, sir," I said, pausing before playing my best hand, "but since I think there is reasonable doubt that the witness can identify the defendant in open court, I'd like to seat him in the spectator area and see if she can pick him out."

"Oh, for Christ's sake," Randall protested. "She doesn't have to do that. She's already properly identified him. Besides, Armstrong's got the court packed with Chicanos."

The judge leaned back in his chair and, after some reflection, said, "I'll hear argument on the motion."

I pulled the file out of my briefcase and began. The long research I had done gave me a strong foundation, and I was beginning to feel confident.

"According to police records, Miss Horn says she was asleep in a dark room at one o'clock in the morning when she was awakened by an intruder. She screamed and turned on a light. The intruder jumped on her, stifled her scream with a pillow, turned out the light and, according to her, raped her. The few seconds that the light was on was the only time she was able to see her attacker. The description she gave the police was of a young, tall, well-built Chicano with a hairline moustache. I can offer unlimited testimony, including Doctor Paley's, if necessary, that the defendant has never worn a moustache of any kind. And the next day the victim sees Rodriguez in the office and tells the doctor that she *thinks* he *might* be the man who raped her. At this point the police are called in, and they present Rodriguez to Miss Horn behind a one-way mirror. It's here that I object. Since she was uncertain about her identification in the doctor's office, we have no way of knowing what the detectives did or said to her to convince her that Rodriguez was indeed the rapist. Why wasn't he given a lawyer to protect his rights during this confrontation? There was no hurry; no dying witness or anything. And if they were so sure of their man, why didn't they put him in a lineup?"

"They don't use lineups anymore," Randall said, "thanks to all the problems *Wade* caused."

"Well, in this case they should have," I argued. "Properly conducted and with a lawyer present, it would at least have given him a chance."

Randall looked exasperated. "Your honor, I think we're getting way off the track. Mr. Armstrong persistently overlooks the fact that we're involved in a simple preliminary hearing. I'm not even going to debate the issue, since it's not relevant."

The judge stroked his beard. "Any more argument, Mr. Armstrong?"

"I'll accept a ruling," I said. "All I know is that my client is a respectable citizen, an employee of the city, who has never been in legal trouble before. One day a girl points her finger at him and he's plucked away from his family and his job and thrown into jail. I plan to test the witness's identification at a later hearing if I have to, but if you allow her to view the defendant in court today, you may reinforce her impression of him and take away that chance. I'm not trying to be technical here; I simply want to give my client every constitutional protection by forcing that girl to be damn sure she's sure."

"So do I," Randall said. "But I don't see the cops as bad guys in this case. They didn't drag Rodriguez into the station on a whim. A rape victim saw him and spontaneously identified him. I see no violation of due process."

The judge stamped out his cigarette in an ashtray and looked up at me. "I refuse the request for an open-court identification, Mr. Armstrong. Some of your argument has merit, but I agree with the prosecutor that you will have ample opportunity to voice this objection at a later hearing." He stood up and added, "I'll return to the bench in a few minutes. Thank you, gentlemen."

I had lost the battle, but the war was still to be won. When I returned to the courtroom and joined Jennifer and the Rodriguez group, I devised another plan. I had read of outlandish tactics lawyers had used to impeach eyewitness testimony, especially in a famous case that F. Lee Bailey had won in Boston, but I had no way of knowing how this particular judge would react. I knew that I would not be placing Ralph in any more jeopardy than he was already in, but the judge could certainly jail me for contempt if he felt like it. Still, I had to do it.

Wendy Horn was already back on the witness stand before the judge noticed that the defendant was once again wearing the paper bag over his head.

"Mr. Armstrong, remove that thing from your

client's head this instant. I don't intend to warn you again. If you continue with this behavior, you risk criminal contempt."

I removed the bag quickly, and the judge said, "You may proceed, Mr. Randall."

Randall began, "Miss Horn, we're all aware of the ordeal you have undergone, and none of us wishes to cause you any unpleasantness by making you relive that night. However, the charge against the defendant is a serious one, and the court wants to do everything in its power to insure against a miscarriage of justice. With that in mind, I'd like to ask you a few questions."

When she nodded, he asked, "Did you initially describe your assailant as wearing a thin moustache?"

"Yes, sir."

"And when you saw the defendant the next day, was he wearing a moustache?"

"No, sir, but one of the detectives told me he might have shaved it off." She seemed nervous, even though she and Randall had obviously rehearsed their dialogue.

"And is it true that when you first saw him in the doctor's office, you weren't positive the defendant was the man who raped you?"

"No, not exactly. I was afraid to look at him there," she explained, "but when I saw him through the one-way mirror I was positive."

"Were you able to get a good look at him that night in your apartment?"

"Just for a moment, when the light was on. But that was a very intense moment. I don't think I'll ever forget it."

Randall paused, then turned to face the defense ta-

38

ble. "All right, Miss Horn. Now I want to know if you can identify the man who raped you. Do you see that man in this courtroom?"

"Yes," she said, nodding toward us. "He's sitting right over there."

"Point him out, please," Randall directed, and when she did, he added, "Very well, let the record indicate . . ."

I did not hear the rest of his sentence. At times during Wendy Horn's testimony I had actually been holding my breath. Now as I gathered the courage to rise, I inhaled and exhaled deeply several times before getting to my feet.

"Excuse me," I said flatly, "but if it please the court, the witness has identified someone other than the accused. This man is not Ralph Rodriguez."

"What?" The judge leaned forward and stared down at Ralph's friend, then rapped his gavel in an attempt to still the noisy murmurs coming from the crowd.

"Is the defendant in the courtroom?" he demanded.

Ralph stood up in the rear of the room.

"Bailiff, bring him back up here and take this man to his seat. And get his name. I want his name."

"Your honor," I said, "I take full responsibility. This man is here at my suggestion."

The judge's face was very red, but he remained silent as Rodriguez was brought back to my table. Randall was still standing, speechless, and Wendy Horn looked bewildered. The rumble of whispers in the courtroom did not subside.

"That's all right," the judge said to the bailiff who was about to take Ralph's friend away. "You can let him go." He sat stroking his beard for what seemed like a long

39

time before he finally turned to Wendy Horn and excused her from the stand. He then motioned for Randall and me to approach the bench.

I began talking as soon as I got there. "Your honor, I sincerely apologize for upsetting the court, but I knew no other way to prove my point. I frankly don't know how far a defense counsel should go in defending his client, but I would go this far again. The sole evidence, the only witness, against the defendant has been shown to be completely unreliable." I stopped talking, hoping for the best, crossing the fingers of both hands behind my back. For all I knew, I might wind up in jail myself.

"I'm not telling you how far you can go, Mr. Armstrong," the judge said evenly and sternly, "but I am telling you that willful obstruction of the orderly processes of this court is grounds for contempt." He paused, then added, "However, this time I will accept it as a mistake and warn you. This time." He turned to Randall. "I'm just as furious as you must be, Mr. Randall, but I can't think of any way to get the toothpaste back into the tube. Can you?"

Randall shook his head. He looked as if somebody had hit him in the stomach.

"Make your motion then, Mr. Armstrong," the judge suggested, and Randall and I returned to our tables.

I looked through the papers in my briefcase for the page on which I had written the exact wording the night before and, finding it, said, "Your honor, at this time the defense would like to move to dismiss all charges against this defendant for failure of the People to show a prima facie case."

The judge picked up his copy of the complaint and stated, just as formally, "There being no sufficient cause to believe the within-named Ralph Rodriguez guilty of the offense charged, I order him to be released."

He banged his gavel one last time, and for the first time in my short career as a lawyer my legs were not shaking. Ralph extended his upturned palms to me and I slapped them, offering him mine in return. His mother and his wife rushed up to embrace him, and I saw Jennifer coming through the crowd toward me. She looked very proud.

Ralph's mother had been crying hysterically, but when we got her into the hallway she composed herself enough to say to me, "Mr. Armstrong, I want to thank you personally and from the bottom of my heart for saving my son. You are a good man."

The friend who had impersonated Ralph in court said, "Mister, you're some kind of a lawyer." He also slapped my palms, as did the four other friends. Casey and Hansen came out of the courtroom, shielding Wendy Horn between them, and rushed her past the crowd. A couple of the spectators even came up to congratulate us, and then Doctor Paley stopped by to inform Ralph that she was happy for him and looked forward to seeing him at work again on Monday morning. Jennifer kissed me again, and finally Ralph suggested that we all go to his favorite restaurant for a celebration.

Everybody agreed. Jennifer and I took Ralph and his wife and his mother in our car. The Old Mexico was just that—old—plus rundown, but it served us fresh and fragrant enchiladas with an unmistakably authentic hot sauce. After a while the conversation drifted into animated Spanish, but throughout the meal Ralph's mother smiled benevolently and thankfully at me.

41

When Jennifer and I had finished eating, I rose and announced that we had a long drive up the coast and would have to leave. I offered to pay our share of the bill, but Ralph waved his arms.

"No way, Mr. Armstrong. This is the least I can do."

I silently agreed, and after more expressions of gratitude all around we left. Inside our car, I kissed Jennifer for a long time before turning on the engine.

"How do you feel after winning your first case?" she asked.

"I'm not sure. I'm glad he's free, but something about that restaurant makes me doubt his innocence. I can't quite put my finger on it, but it's bothering me."

"Well, I think you were magnificent in court, and I also think Ralph Rodriguez is one very lucky man."

I kissed her once more before heading the car toward Bodega Bay. The rain had been blown out to sea, leaving behind an azure sky, and we decided to take the longer but more beautiful route along the coast highway.

Bodega Bay was a cluster of buildings and homes facing the sea. Although a couple of places in town that catered to visitors in the summer were scrubbed and freshly painted, in general it appeared as weatherworn and workmanlike as the fishermen who were its principal residents.

Abe's garage and house was a two-level structure thrown against the side of a sheer hill overlooking the bay. The upper part of the building was level with the road leading into town. A sign retained from a previous owner still read, A&G GARAGE.

There were three cars in various stages of recovery here, along with a magnificent 1938 Phantom III Rolls Royce limousine, which was one of the few possessions I had retained from my previous marriage. A year ago

Abe had paid the past-due storage bills and had it shipped from New York. In addition to the major engine work, the car needed interior and exterior care, and under Abe's supervision Jennifer and I had spent several weekends helping him restore some of its lost glamour. Although there were many work hours ahead of us, we enjoyed the car anyway, and on the previous Saturday we had relaxed at the end of the day, Jennifer and I in the rear, Abe in the chauffeur's compartment with the window divider down, sipping scotch from the crystal decanter out of the rosewood bar, pretending we had already finished our task and were cruising Golden Gate Park on a sunny Sunday.

This Saturday Abe and I were up early enjoying the view from the kitchen–living room. This portion of the building was beneath the garage and consisted of three large rooms in a row, all of them facing a deck which ran the length of the rooms, overlooking the water. Jennifer and I had spent the previous evening telling Abe all about the events at the trial, but he was still questioning me as we lingered over our coffee. He was very happy for me, but he also wanted me to try to keep the whole thing in perspective.

"Pride," he said, waving his finger back and forth. "Don't let pride carry you away. Keep your head clear so you can help anybody else the way you helped Rodriguez."

I smiled agreement, then changed the subject. "Do you want to work on the Rolls today?" I asked, taking a sip of hot coffee.

Abe shook his head. He was eating his usual breakfast of toast, cottage cheese, jam and sliced fruit. Although he always made it look incredibly appetizing, I could not eat anything until after several cups of coffee.

"No," Abe answered, "I thought we'd go fishing. I've got a transmission job to finish, but I should be through by noon. While I'm doing that, you and Jennifer could get the boat ready."

"Great," I said, "but how will we get Jennifer out of bed? We were up very late talking."

Abe rose. "We'll use the patented recipe."

The thought of that made even me hungry, and we sprang into action. While Abe started butter melting in a pan on the stove, I chopped onions, green peppers and celery. Years ago I had become aware that Abe fully accepted me as a son when he allowed me to assist him with his legendary dish, taking me on as a confidential apprentice. When I had finished the chopping, we threw the results into the melted butter, added garlic, cayenne pepper and oregano in bulk, than a dash of most of the other spices in his cupboard, put the top on the pan and let it simmer. The aroma was heavenly.

I went into the bedroom and stood next to the bed. After a few seconds the odor began to waft back, and Jennifer opened her eyes slowly.

"Do I smell Abe's eggs and onions?" she asked.

I nodded and leaned over, kissing her softly on the face and neck.

"How many eggs?" she demanded with mock seriousness.

"A dozen," I answered. "That's all we had."

"Twelve is hardly worth getting up for," she said, tossing her long hair away from her face, "but don't you dare start without me."

I returned to the front room and told Abe, "It works every time. She'll be right out."

We ate all of the eggs, half of the pan's contents going to Jennifer. Abe and I divided the other half. I commented on Jennifer's appetite as she finished even the burned scrapings, and I suggested that the one who had eaten the most should do the dishes. She accepted the chore without protest, and Abe and I went upstairs to the garage.

I tinkered with the Rolls while Abe worked on one of his customers' cars. As soon as Jennifer was finished with the dishes, she and I would go to the dock to get the boat ready. Abe and I had been in the garage only a few minutes when she frantically called us back downstairs. "What's wrong?" I asked, running into the room. I was afraid she had cut or burned herself.

Jennifer pointed to the radio, but all I heard was a weather forecast.

"It was just on the news," she cried excitedly. "Wendy Horn was murdered. Last night. By the Bay Ripper." She hugged herself as though she felt suddenly bare.

"Oh, no," I moaned, shaking my head. I took Jennifer in my arms, and she reached up to touch my face.

"But that's not all, David. They arrested him. They say he's the Bay Ripper."

"Rodriguez?" I asked.

"Rodriguez."

I went immediately to the telephone and told the operator to get me the San Francisco police. When I was eventually connected to the Inspectors Bureau, I asked to speak to Casey. When the voice on the other end of the phone told me he was not in, I said, "This is David Armstrong. I'm the attorney for Ralph Rodriguez, and I want to give you some instructions. But please give me your name again."

After I wrote down the name, I continued: "Tell Inspector Casey I'm not in town but I'm on my way to

46

the Hall of Justice. I don't want my client questioned until I get there, and I don't want any evidence of any kind taken until I'm present. Do you understand that?"

The detective said he would relay the message, and I hung up. Abe and Jennifer still stood in the middle of the room. I went over and kissed Jennifer good-by, then turned to Abe.

"Can you drive her home after you finish the car?" I asked.

He assured me he would, and with their blessings I headed back to the city. I left the coast and took the turnoff to Sebastopol, where I could intercept the freeway, but the trip would still take at least an hour and a half. The radio's FM signal was weak that far from the city, so I tuned in a middle-of-the-road AM station and watched the dairy landscape blur past. It was a bright, sunny day, and I would usually have enjoyed the ride, but today I wished fervently that I had stayed in Sausalito.

I tried to take in the knowledge of Wendy Horn's death and of Rodriguez as the murderer. What could possibly have occurred since I had last seen them both? My thoughts were interrupted every few minutes by news bulletins announcing the Bay Ripper's capture.

The District Attorney and the Chief of Police had just concluded a joint news conference in which the Chief had said, "We're sure we have the right man. There is conclusive evidence which we plan to present to the Grand Jury Monday morning. There will be no more so-called Ripper murders."

I wondered how anybody accused of a crime could ever get a fair trial after a statement like that. Although the role of the news media bothered me, I knew the real

47

fault was not there, and in any case I could not justify censorship. My complaint was with the police. The Supreme Court consistently overturned convictions because of improper and excessive pretrial publicity, yet the police never learned. It seemed the very people we employed to enforce our laws understood them less—or believed in them less—than most citizens. From the tone of his statements on the radio, the police chief appeared thoroughly convinced that the apprehension of Rodriguez was the beginning and the end of the system. The trial and the hearings to come would be just so much gobbledygook intended to delay and complicate, to let a guilty man go free. The more I thought about it, the more I realized what kind of battle faced me. I doubted if, except for myself and Ralph's friends and family, there were half a dozen people in the whole state who still presumed him innocent.

When I finally arrived in downtown San Francisco it was past noon, and I went directly to the Hall of Justice, parking easily in front of the building on the almost deserted street.

After identifying myself and submitting to a search in the lobby, I took the special elevator to the floor of the building occupied by the City Prison. Since it was a weekend, lots of wives and mothers were visiting, sitting in a long row behind a plexiglass divider separating them from the prisoners, with whom they were allowed to communicate only through individual telephone receivers. I was thankful that lawyers were provided private interview rooms, and I waited in the one assigned to me.

When Ralph was brought into the room, he was

dressed in denim clothing and wearing shoes with no laces and without socks. He looked pale and exhausted and, I thought, thoroughly defeated.

"I tried to get you," he said meekly. "I tried seven or eight times, but there was no answer."

"I know; I was out of town. But I'm here now. Tell me what happened." I had taken a couple of packs of Jennifer's cigarettes with me, and I shoved them across the table to him.

He looked at the cigarettes but did not take one. He just kept shaking his head back and forth. "It's too late, Mr. Armstrong. They know too much."

"They questioned you?"

"Questioned me? Man, they beat the shit out of me. They've been beating me since they picked me up." He dropped his head into his arms and sobbed.

I waited for a few moments, then reached across and gripped his shoulder. "I know it was rough, Ralph, but you've got a lot to tell me. Let's begin with what you did after I left you yesterday."

I took out a cigarette and handed it to him. After I lit it, he told me he had stayed at the Old Mexico another hour or so after Jennifer and I left. He took his wife and mother home, dropped two of his friends off on Mission Street, and went to play pool and drink beer with the other three. He said he had returned home about ten-thirty or eleven.

It sounded to me like a weak alibi, but I took down the names and addresses of his friends anyway. "What happened next?"

"Inspector Hansen was waiting on the street when I got home."

"Did he arrest you?"

"No, not exactly. He said he wanted to talk to me downtown and told me to follow him in my van. We went down Mission until we got to the waterfront. I was upset and didn't really think about where we were going until we got to the Marina. He stopped his car and ran back to the van. He pulled me out and handcuffed me, and the next thing I knew there were cops everywhere. I heard him tell the other cops he had found me there, parked across the street from where that girl was killed."

Ralph's composure threatened to desert him again, but I waited him out this time.

"I told Hansen I wouldn't say anything until you got here," he continued, "but he just took me into a little room and beat the hell out of me. He hit me in the nuts, the shins, the gut. Everywhere."

"I don't see any marks on your face," I observed. "How about your body?"

Ralph shook his head. "He didn't leave any. He told me he could beat a man to a pulp and not leave a trace."

"Were any other cops around when he was hitting you?"

"No, just him. He hit me in the gut so much I started throwing up, and another guy brought in a mop and bucket, but he left. Hansen made me clean it up, and he took the bucket away and left me alone for a while. When he came back he told me I'd better be ready to tell him what he wanted. I said I still wanted to wait for you, and he got real mad. He handcuffed me to a chair and cut some of my hair off. For evidence, he said. Then he said he needed some dirt from underneath my finger-nails, and he shoved the blade of his knife right up my nail."

50

Ralph offered his right hand for inspection, and I saw that his forefinger was inflamed and badly swollen. He started to shiver as he recalled the incident.

"And then . . . and then he acted like he was going to take my dick out of my pants. He said, 'Don't cry like a baby, now. I just want to cut off a little piece for evidence.' I started screaming and yelling at the top of my voice, Mr. Armstrong. I begged him. I told him I would say anything he wanted."

His account, true or not, caused him to shake so violently I was afraid he might be in shock. I opened the door and asked one of the deputies to bring a blanket, which he did. I draped the blanket around Ralph's shoulders and put another cigarette in his mouth, lighting it for him. The tobacco seemed to revive him enough for me to continue the questioning.

"So what did you tell them?"

"Everything. Hansen asked me all kind of questions, and I just agreed with anything he said. Then he told me I could call you while he typed it up. But he said it wouldn't do any good. He said he had found out about your police record and he was going to have you disbarred."

I lit my pipe to conceal my anger and tried to reassure Rodriguez through the smoke.

"Look, Ralph, I told you the first time I met you I had been in trouble once myself. But don't worry about me. I'm clean." I hesitated, trying to remain calm. "What happened next?"

"He let me out of the room and told me I could make one phone call, but, like I said, there was no answer. Some guy was waiting for him, though, so I kept calling you while they argued."

51

"Argued? About what?" I asked.

"I don't know. The guy was really pissed. He said he was going to report Hansen to the Commissioner. I think his name was Bell. Hansen just walked away from him and came back and got me."

"And did you sign the statement?"

"I had to, Mr. Armstrong. I didn't know what to do. I couldn't reach you, and I've never been so scared in my life. I . . ."

"Hold on," I interrupted. "I'm not blaming you. I just want to find out what happened. Now, let's take it slowly, and you tell me what's in that statement."

"He found out about the cleaning business," he said, inhaling his cigarette and looking away from me. "He found out I wasn't doing it. My dad left me the business, but I never wanted any part of it. When Momma and Anna thought I was out scrubbing floors, I was breaking into apartments. I had to get more money somehow or they would have known. That's all I was doing in that girl's place when she woke up and surprised me."

"Wendy Horn's place? Last night?"

Rodriguez turned back toward me. "No, no. Last Saturday night. I'm sorry I lied to you, Mr. Armstrong, but I never meant to rape her. I was looking for something to hock, but she was just lying there in bed wearing nothing but panties. And she was beautiful. You saw her. Really beautiful, with long hair and long legs. She screamed, and I threw a pillow over her face until I could turn off the light. I would have gone then, but she was moving her tits against me and getting me excited. She kept begging me not to rape her so much, that's all I could think of. I hadn't planned it, but she wanted it. You know what I mean. It just happened. It was over quick and I left."

52

I hoped my face did not reveal the disgust I felt. I knew I would get little else out of him if he sensed I was judging him, so I said, "I understand, Ralph. In fact, I knew you were lying about the rape."

He seemed amazed. "How?"

"I should have realized it yesterday at the Old Mexico," I explained, "but it didn't really dawn on me until today, driving here. You told me you had been working there the night she was raped, but that place hasn't been cleaned in years, much less polished."

Ralph remained slumped in his chair, his features shrouded in gloom.

"Come on," I coaxed. "You've admitted the rape, so tell me the whole thing. Once and for all. Get it out."

He continued staring at the floor. "It's bad. Worse than you think. They're going to pin the Ripper murders on me. They found a list next to her body, and they said I had her panties in my van."

"What kind of list?" I asked.

"I don't know. Hansen said it was a list from my office with her name on it."

"From the Health Department?"

He nodded.

"Did you have her panties in the van from the time you raped her?"

"No, sir. I never took any panties, and I don't know what list he's talking about. I didn't kill anybody."

He started to break down again, but I stopped him by slamming my pipe on the table.

"Then why did you sign a confession?"

"I had to, Mr. Armstrong. He told me he'd kill me if I didn't sign it. He said I was crazy if I thought he was going to let somebody like me run around loose. He said he'd find me when he was off duty and kill me with his bare hands if he had to. I believed him, but, Jesus Christ, I'm not the Bay Ripper. You've got to make them see that."

I hesitated before answering, reflecting on everything he had told me. I realized that I had successfully defended him against a charge he now admitted, but I doubted if I would be so lucky again. Furthermore, I was not at all sure he was telling me the truth this time.

"I think you must know from the first trial that I'll do everything I possibly can for you, Ralph, but I don't want to mislead you. We've got a tough fight ahead of us. Right now I just want you to go back to your cell and get some rest, and I'll see that you receive some medical attention for that finger."

I led him out of the room and returned him to his jailers, leaving instructions with the deputy in charge to have him fed and examined. I rode the special elevator back downstairs, walked across the lobby, and took the regular elevator up to the Inspectors Bureau.

Casey was not in, but Hansen was. He presented himself to me wearing the same gray suit I had seen in court. He looked as if he hadn't slept in days.

"I'm David Armstrong," I said. "From the Rodriguez case. Do you remember?"

"Yeah. What can I do for you?"

"First of all, I want to congratulate you. I'll defend my client no matter what, but if he really is the Bay Ripper, I'm as happy as you are that you've caught him."

"I'm not buying that crap. What else do you want?"

I shrugged and said, "Okay. Just give me the details of the crime. You know, time, place, et cetera."

"Haven't you talked to Rodriguez?"

"Not yet," I lied. "I was out of town for the weekend,

and I came straight here when I heard the news on the radio. I'd like to find out what's up before I question him."

Hansen said, "Okay, but I won't tell you anything more than you can find out in the papers. I discovered her body last night about ten-thirty. She had been killed like all the others—ripped wide open. The coroner says she had been dead less than an hour when I found her."

"How did you happen on her body?"

"I took her home after the rape hearing. She was upset about the charges being dropped and afraid to go back to her own apartment after her name had come out. She had a key to an aunt's house in the Marina, so I took her there. Her aunt was out of the country—Spain or somewhere. I was worried about her being alone there, and when I checked back later in the evening I found her lying on the bed, laid out like a slaughtered animal. And the first thing I saw when I went outside to look around was your boy, Rodriguez, sitting in his van across the street from the house." He paused, then added, "The rest you'll have to find out in court."

"Did you ask his friends to verify his story? He was with me from the hearing until after three o'clock, and he says he went drinking with his friends until ten-thirty."

Hansen's eyes flashed with anger at the realization that I had already talked with Rodriguez.

"He said a lot of things, Mr. Armstrong. But he can't prove anything. We can. But, like I said, you'll have to find that out in court."

When he started to walk away, I said, very politely, "Just one more question, if you don't mind, Inspector. Do you make it a practice to slander attorneys?"

"What are you talking about?"

"I understand you told Rodriguez you were going to have me disbarred," I said evenly.

Hansen's face reddened, the rage rushing to the tip of his nose and bulging out his eyes. Suddenly I was aware of the other detectives in the room watching us, and I felt the kind of fear Ralph must have felt being at the mercy of these people. But I remembered that I was not in custody; that, somehow, despite all the mess in my past and despite all the odds and the rules, I had edged inside, just a little. No matter how hollow it sounded to part of me, I was an officer of the court, and I planned to take advantage of it.

"You may have checked my police record, Inspector, but you didn't check far enough. It's true I was convicted of a crime in New York years ago, but the court eventually dismissed the indictment. Do you know what that means?"

He did not reply, and I answered for him. "It means it's even better than a pardon. They withdrew the conviction. It never legally happened. And when you called me a convicted felon, you slandered me, mister. Slandered me to a client and disparaged me in my profession."

Confusion clouded over the fading fury on Hansen's face. I stepped back, prepared to leave, but my own anger had taken over, and I said, in a louder voice for the benefit of anyone else in the room, "So may God and whatever benevolent association you belong to have mercy, because Monday morning I am going to sue you for everything you have or ever will have. Your home, your car, your TV set, your kids' bikes, everything, Inspector. And that's only the beginning. If what my client tells me is true and you tortured a confession out of him last night and planted evidence on him, then I'll also have your ass. I don't know what kind of lawyers you've come up against in the past, but I'll promise you this. You'd rather lose your arms and legs than have me as an enemy."

I walked out to find a gray skirt of fog wriggling its way around the city. I was extremely agitated still, but I knew where I was going. I went directly to the Marina.

A section of five blocks or so, the Marina contains some of San Francisco's most expensive mansions. Although the houses vary in size and elegance, most are two-storied, and each has at least one room fully glassed from floor to ceiling to take advantage of the view; a green park, the harbor, Alcatraz Island, and the full bay. The green between the houses and the water was filled this Saturday, as always on weekends, with people sightseeing; with kids tossing frisbees; with couples, young and old, strolling; and with countless unleashed dogs leaping and yelping at each other. The fog was rolling in very quickly, but there were still a few girls lying on the grass, absorbing the last of the sun.

I parked the car in front of one of the pay telescopes and walked across the park, looking up at the houses. No matter what time of day or night I came here, the windows were always undraped, and I wondered if anybody had seen Hansen arrest Ralph last night. Two uniformed policemen stood outside a pink stucco house on the corner, and barricades surrounded the small lawn. A group of people had congregated on the sidewalk, trying to see something, but the windows were draped and the doors closed.

It occurred to me to try to bluff my way past the

guards somehow, but I thought better of it and simply stood with the rest of the curious until the front door opened and several men came out of the house. One of the men was Inspector Casey, and I went up to him as he headed for a waiting police car.

"Can I speak with you a moment, Inspector?"

He hesitated while the other men got into the car. "You're the attorney, aren't you? Mr.—?"

"Armstrong," I offered.

"Right. I'm in a hurry now, Mr. Armstrong. Why don't you call me in the office in a few hours? Sorry." He bent over and asked someone, "Which hotel is Pell staying at?" and a voice answered, "The Fairmount." Casey slammed the door as the car sped away.

I glanced at my watch and, seeing that it was past four, decided to go home. The Marina was at the foot of the Golden Gate Bridge, so Sausalito was only a few minutes away. As I walked toward the car, I couldn't get Pell's name out of my mind. I had first seen it on the mailbox that night in front of Wendy Horn's apartment, and then the police report had said that her boyfriend, an Anthony Pell, had been interviewed after the rape. I wondered where he had been the night of the attack and why he was staying in a hotel when he shared an apartment with Wendy Horn. And most of all, I wanted to know why Inspector Casey wanted to talk to him.

I ran the rest of the way to the car. From a nearby telephone booth I called the Fairmount Hotel.

"Mr. Pell's room, please," I told the hotel clerk.

There was a secondary ring, and then a male voice answered, "Yes?"

"Mr. Pell?"

"No. Who's calling?"

"This is Chief of Police Wilson," I said. "Inspector Casey has been delayed, and he asked me to call to see if there's anything I can do. Can we handle it on the phone?"

"I'm John Lawrence, Mr. Pell's attorney," the voice said. "As we told the Inspector, we want to avoid publicity if we can, but Mr. Pell is adamant about pressing charges against that detective. We don't care who it is, but somebody in authority had better get over here soon. Mr. Pell is quite upset."

I didn't know what to say without making him suspicious, so I simply asked, "What detective, Mr. Lawrence?"

"Hansen," he said. "The one Miss Horn complained about. I thought you said you had talked with Inspector Casey. Did you say this was Chief Wilson?"

"Yes," I said. "Chief of Police Wilson." I hung up. My thoughts raced as I went to the car. Hansen. Pell. Wendy Horn. So Pell was the "Mr. Bell" whom Rodriguez had seen arguing with Hansen at the police station. But I still could not imagine what was bothering Pell so much that he wanted to prosecute Hansen.

As I drove across the bridge, I considered having a steam beer at the No Name Bar, but I decided against it when I saw the usual throng of weekend visitors crowding into the little town. Instead I picked up a six pack at the corner store and went to the apartment.

Abe and Jennifer still had not arrived, so I took a beer onto the terrace and sat down, hoping that the late-afternoon sun and the tranquillity would help me decide what to do next. I had made little progress when the telephone rang.

It was Casey. "I just got to Mr. Pell's room, Armstrong, and I'd like to know if you're the mysterious Chief of Police who called."

I did not answer immediately, and Casey persisted. "Listen, I'm not going to do anything about it, but I have to find out. I can't think of anybody else who knew where I was going, but if you didn't call, it was a reporter. And if it was a reporter . . ."

"I won't say who called, Inspector," I said, "but I can assure you it was not a reporter."

He accepted that, and the whole tone of his voice changed. "I don't know how much you found out, Armstrong, but I would personally appreciate it if you wouldn't say anything to anybody, especially the press, until I've had a chance to talk with you."

"All right," I said slowly, not sure what he was up to.

"In fact," Casey continued, "I'm tied up today, but I'd like to talk with you tomorrow in your home, if that's all right. You live in Sausalito, don't you?"

"Yes," I admitted, then asked, "How did you know? Where did you get my number?"

"From Rodriguez. I called the jail and had them find out for me. Will it be all right if I stop by tomorrow afternoon? Around one?"

"Sure," I said. "I'll be here."

Casey's manner had been so accommodating that I wondered what I had uncovered by that phone call to Pell. I opened the door and picked up the afternoon paper before returning to the terrace. The front page was covered with pictures of Wendy Horn and stories about the case. I read the articles, drank my beer, and waited for Abe and Jennifer.

Casey rang our doorbell at precisely one o'clock on Sunday afternoon. Abe, Jennifer and I had just finished brunch, and the smell of bagels, cream cheese, lox and sable, tomato and red onion must have assaulted his nose as he walked into the apartment. Jennifer quickly gathered up the scattered sections of the *Chronicle* and the *New York Times* as I introduced Casey to her and Abe.

"Have a seat," I said, offering him the large leather chair I had been occupying. "I'm having a beer. Would you like one?"

Casey hesitated briefly, then accepted, and I went into the kitchen and poured some Coors into two iced mugs I used only for guests. Only a breakfast bar separated the kitchen from the living room, and I could hear

Abe already engaging Casey in conversation. Abe was the most inquisitive and open-minded person I had ever met, and his genuine interest in people disarmed them. By the time I returned with the beer, he had discovered that Casey was an only child and that he had never married.

"And what did your father do for a living, Inspector?" Abe was perched on a footstool facing Casey, and I thought he looked like a little bird as he pecked away with his questions.

"He was a watchmaker, Mr. Davidson," said Casey with a touch of impatience. "Why do you ask?"

"No particular reason," Abe replied, smiling warmly at him. "Just getting to know you."

Casey turned to me. "Is there someplace we can talk, Mr. Armstrong?"

"Right here," I said. "There's nothing we can't discuss in front of these two."

"All right. I want to know what you plan to do now that you've learned about Mr. Pell's complaint against Hansen."

"I'm not sure yet. Before I make a decision, I'd like to know more about what happened, but I'm prepared to subpoena Pell to get the details if I have to."

Casey sighed. "That's what I was afraid of, and that's why I'm here. I hope I can persuade you to keep the whole thing out of the trial and out of the papers." He lighted a cigarette and sampled his beer before continuing. "Mr. Pell and Miss Horn had been living together, but they had a fight the night she was raped, and he moved into the Fairmount. She didn't want to go back to the apartment after the hearing Friday, so Hansen took her to an aunt's house and stayed with her for

62

several hours. Later in the evening she called Pell at the hotel and complained that Hansen was making sexual advances to her. Pell went to the house, and Hansen took him to a neighborhood bar, trying to calm him down. When Hansen got back to the house a couple of hours later, he found Wendy Horn's body. I'm the first to admit that Hansen's behavior is appalling, but it had nothing to do with that girl's death. He's a career cop with a fine record, but you can imagine what this would do to him if it's brought out in the midst of the trial. I've been able to get Mr. Pell's promise to keep this under his hat on my personal guarantee that Hansen will be dealt with severely, by the department, in our own way. I'd like your agreement also, Mr. Armstrong."

"Inspector, I don't know if you're aware of it or not, but that man tried to discredit me by telling my client I had a police record. Furthermore, his story of the arrest and interrogation is widely at variance with Rodriguez's. And now I find out that he tried to seduce a rape victim placed in his care. Frankly, Inspector, I don't share your concern for Mr. Hansen. I plan to sue him for millions and to do everything in my power to destroy him."

Casey responded very deliberately: "We're not in total disagreement, Mr. Armstrong. If you think Hansen slandered you, that's for the courts to decide. And if you have proof that he beat up Rodriguez, any judge will throw out the confession. All I'm asking is that you don't bring out this sex thing in the middle of the Bay Ripper clamor. This trial is going to generate a lot of publicity, and you'll be trying Hansen in the papers just as surely as you lawyers are always claiming we do with your clients."

I was impressed by his logic, but I still did not yield the point.

"There's one other thing," Casey added. "Let's just say it's also to our mutual advantage to cooperate. You're a new criminal attorney in town, and I'm Chief of Inspectors. It wouldn't hurt you to be owed a favor by me."

I had to smile, as did Jennifer and Abe, and I said, "I'll agree to this much—I'll talk to Pell, and if what you say is true, if his testimony would not help the defense, I won't call him and I won't say anything to the press. Fair enough?"

"Fair enough," Casey said and raised his mug. "You might uncover some dirt, but I assure you none of it has anything to do with the murder, and it can't help your client. We have an airtight case against Rodriguez."

Jennifer stood up. "I'm sorry, Inspector. I should have offered before, but there's plenty of food left on the table if you're hungry."

"No, thanks, Mrs. Armstrong. I have to be going."

"It'll only take a second to toast a bagel," I prodded. "How about some smoked sable with a little cream cheese and tomato?"

Jennifer took his hesitation to mean acceptance and began preparing the snack. Casey took a sip of beer and looked around the room, complimenting us on our apartment and the view.

"Thank you," I said. I decided to take advantage of the harmonious mood. "What exactly do you have on Rodriguez, Inspector? I don't expect you to divulge all your evidence, but I hardly think a disputed confession is an airtight case."

Casey grinned at my artless approach but was able to

avoid an answer when Jennifer brought a plate to him. While he ate his bagel, I stuffed some newspapers beneath the cold logs in the fireplace and lighted them; then I went into the kitchen and brought back two more beers. Casey finished his bagel, handed the plate back to Jennifer, thanked her, and stared into the now crackling fire before responding to my earlier question.

"You're right, Mr. Armstrong. I'm not going to get into all the evidence, but I appreciate your help on this Hansen situation, so I'll tell you generally what we've got. The D.A.'s presenting it to the Grand Jury tomorrow anyway."

He paused to light a cigarette, then went on. "Counting Wendy Horn, we think there have been eight killings, all committed by the same person. The first victim was a nineteen-year-old college girl around the beginning of the year. We hadn't heard from the Zodiac in quite a while, and everybody thought he was operating again. But it turned out not to be his m.o. at all, so we treated it as a routine homicide. Then another young girl was killed the same way about a month later in Pacific Heights. Ripped open. The newspapers still hadn't picked up on it, but we knew we had another mass murderer on our hands, and, what with the Zodiac and the Zebra killings, we had already had enough for a lifetime. When we found the next victim, the press got involved and invented the name Bay Ripper, and we've had at least one murder a month of that type ever since. The victims were all young girls, usually living alone. No signs of forced entry or struggle, although every one of them had traces of a knockout drug in her body. All the murders were committed at night, and no one ever reported hearing any screams. And all the girls were pretty. Each of them could be classified as very pretty."

"They were all raped, too, weren't they?" I suggested.

Casey shook his head. "The news media started that, but we honestly don't know for sure. Each of the bodies suffered massive damage to the vagina, but there was never any trace of semen. Whether they were actually raped or not, their sexual organs were certainly attacked. The breasts and lower body were slashed, and one girl's uterus was actually removed."

"Were the cuts surgically proficient, Inspector?"

"There's no way to tell, Mr. Armstrong. They were certainly done with a sharp instrument, but the wounds were so deep and wide that it was impossible to determine. Those girls were simply disemboweled."

Suddenly aware of the impact his descriptions were having on all of us, he apologized only to Jennifer.

"I'm sorry, Mrs. Armstrong."

"I'm sorry too," Jennifer said. "For those girls."

We all remained silent for a few moments, letting the popping fire fill the void, until Casey said, "You just can't imagine what the bastard did to those girls." He tossed his cigarette butt into the fireplace and turned to me. "And I'm afraid the bastard who did it is your client, Mr. Armstrong."

"What if the judge throws out the confession?" I asked gingerly.

"We don't even need the confession, now that we have the list."

"The list that was found next to Wendy Horn's body?"

"That's right. It had been torn out of a cross-reference telephone directory, the kind that lists the number first, then tells you the name and address of the person who has it. Wendy Horn's aunt's was one of the names on that list, and Hansen found the book it had been torn out of at the Rape Bureau. They used it when the girls who called in were so hysterical that all they could get out of them was a telephone number. You may have a beef with Inspector Hansen, Mr. Armstrong, but he used that list to crack this case wide open. He went through the files and discovered that every one of the Bay Ripper victims had been a patient at the Rape Bureau. All within the last year."

"That still doesn't mean . . ." I started to object, but Casey interrupted me.

"It simply means that Rodriguez is the only guy in the whole city who could have known all those girls."

"What you're saying is very incriminating," I admitted, "but he's not the only person working there. If all those girls were patients at the Rape Bureau, as you say, how come somebody there didn't realize the connection before? There's been too much publicity. It doesn't make sense."

"That bothered us also," Casey said, "at first. But none of the volunteers worked regularly enough to have known each of the victims. And they never saw the patients anyway. They just answered the telephone. As for Doctor Paley, she's literally on call around the clock. She said she doesn't subscribe to a newspaper and hasn't had time to read one in years. Until Rodriguez was arrested, she wasn't even aware of the Bay Ripper case. She spends whatever free time she has caring for her invalid father, who lives with her."

Casey thought a moment before speaking again. "You had me over the barrel with this Pell and Hansen thing, Mr. Armstrong, and you didn't take advantage of me, so I'll be frank with you. I told you before that we didn't know for sure if those girls had been raped or not, and we didn't—in the first seven cases. But we found semen in Wendy Horn's body. We're still investigating everyone connected with that Bureau, but Rodriguez was the only man working there. You beat the rap on Friday, but you and I both know he's still a rapist. When you combine that with the fact that he had knowledge of all the victims and was found at the scene of Wendy Horn's murder with a pair of her panties in his possession, you have what I call an airtight case. I'm sure you'll see that Rodriguez gets his day in court, Mr. Armstrong, but I'm just as certain that he'll go to the gas chamber."

I was overwhelmed by the information, and when I did not immediately respond, Casey turned to Abe.

"You know, Mr. Davidson, I've been involved in homicides for eighteen years and I've seen a lot of things, but this kind of senseless killing still drives me up the wall. You said you were an analyst. Does it make any sense to you?"

"Not a bit, Inspector, but I'm only an amateur psychologist. My profession is automobile mechanics."

"Some of your customers think it's exactly the opposite," Jennifer said. "They bring their cars in and can't get away until they've told you their life's story."

"Perhaps," Abe granted. He leaned forward in his chair facing Casey and said, "I have no theories that might help you, Inspector. When I'm repairing a car, I can usually tell what's wrong with it simply by observing and listening. You know, if it's missing, that it's the plugs. If the exhaust is dark and thick, it needs rings. But people are just not that transparent. Obviously murderers look and behave just like everybody else. Otherwise, your job would be a lot easier."

Casey nodded vigorously and said, "I can't tell you how glad I am to hear somebody say that. We've been deluged with experts offering solutions ever since this case broke. Psychiatrists, medical anthropologists, chemists, graphologists, astrologers. Even a psychic. I think if I could weigh all the nonsense they've given me, it would sink a battleship."

"Yes," Abe said, "I'm afraid experts often deal in stereotypes. They give you a profile of a typical killer and think all you have to do is match it up to a suspect. As you know, that isn't much help. Dividing people into types is just not informative. I've only just met you, but already I know you're not a typical policeman. I'm not a typical mechanic; Jennifer is not a typical dancer; and, as you must have already discovered, David is not a typical lawyer. In the psychology I practice, it's important to find out a person's life style, based on early recollections, and whether he has basically an external or an internal personality. I also like to find out whether he is the oldest, the youngest or an only child. That's why I was asking you all those questions earlier. But even when I know all that about a person, it's the merest beginning. The road leading to understanding another human being is a long one. It's almost as long as the one leading to an understanding of ourselves."

Casey looked at his watch and drained the last of the beer from his mug.

"I've really enjoyed talking to you, Mr. Davidson, but I've got to get going." He stood up to thank Jennifer, then turned to me.

I stood also and said, "I'm aware that you don't normally go around laying out your evidence for defense attorneys, Inspector, and I appreciate it. I'll talk to Pell tomorrow, and if everything is as you say it is, I'll keep my bargain."

Casey nodded and said, "I hope all your cases aren't this hopeless, Armstrong. This one stinks, and I don't envy you."

I did not sense any sarcasm in the remark, and we shook hands warmly before I let him out the front door. Abe helped Jennifer clear the dishes from the table, and I returned to the floor in front of the fireplace, trying to poke some life into the smoldering logs as I pondered the possible consequences of Casey's charges. Jennifer and I had often discussed, usually heatedly, the propriety of a lawyer's defending a man he knew to be guilty, especially a man guilty of a heinous crime. I had given her books to read and had thrown all of my heroes at her—from John Adams through Clarence Darrow to Melvin Belli and F. Lee Bailey—but I doubted that I had ever made her fully understand my concept of a defense attorney. Everyone believed in some exceptions to justice, but I believed that all, not just some, cases were exceptions; that no one was so despicable that something good could not be said in his defense. Today, however, my vision was clouded with images of Ralph Rodriguez cutting, raping and slashing the bodies of eight young girls, and I wondered how much enthusiasm I actually had for the task ahead of me.

Abe and Jennifer must have sensed my predicament, for I was suddenly aware that both of them were standing over me. Jennifer put her hands out to help me up, and Abe said, "It's a dirty business, David, but you asked for it. What can we do to help you?"

70

"I really don't know," I said honestly. "I'll interview Pell tomorrow and try to check out Rodriguez's alibi with his friends and then come up with some kind of defense. But, as Casey said, it looks like an airtight case."

"Well," Abe said, "the Inspector seems like a very thorough fellow, but what he says may be only partially true. I'll stay over tomorrow, and we'll see what we can find out. While you're talking to Mr. Pell, I'll run down Rodriguez's friends. Then maybe we can both call on Doctor Paley. Okay?"

"Sure," I said gladly.

Abe smiled and said, "Good. Come on over to the table. We've made some tea."

I returned his smile and adopted his enthusiasm. If Ralph Rodriguez was the Bay Ripper, he was still going to get the kind of defense I had always dreamed about giving. I mentally chastised myself for ever doubting it.

8

I called Pell's hotel early Monday morning, but the operator said that Pell had left instructions not to be disturbed until after ten o'clock, so I went to the Hall of Justice to see Ralph. After taking Jennifer to school, Abe was going to find out what Ralph's three friends could tell us, then meet me back in the apartment before three in the afternoon.

"How are you feeling?" I asked Ralph as the deputy brought him into the interview room at the jail.

"Pretty good. They sent a doctor up after you were here last. He put some stuff on my finger and gave me a sleeping pill, but he made me take off all my clothes and took pictures. To prove there were no bruises, I guess."

"I guess," I said. "Are they allowing you visitors?"

"Yeah. Momma and Anna were here yesterday."

"How are they taking all this?"

"Pretty good. Momma's already been to the Mexican-American Defense League and asked them to help us raise bail. How much do you think we'll have to come up with?"

I told him the truth. "They're not going to let you out on bail, Ralph. I'm telling you this straight out because I don't want you to be surprised by anything. The District Attorney is bringing down an indictment for eight first-degree murders, and he'll ask for the death penalty."

Ralph cringed as he lit another cigarette with the butt of one still burning.

I continued: "I had a long talk with Inspector Casey yesterday, and he told me what they've got on you. They can place you at the scene of Wendy Horn's murder. They found her panties in your van. And the list that was next to her body was torn from a telephone directory in your office, and they discovered that not only Wendy Horn but all of the Bay Ripper victims had been in contact with the Rape Bureau. If that isn't enough, they've got your confession."

"You think I'm guilty too, don't you, Mr. Armstrong?" Ralph asked quietly. "Everybody thinks I'm the Bay Ripper. These deputies, and the other guys locked up in here. I can see it in their eyes. Nobody will talk to me. Momma and Anna try to hide it, but I can see the doubt in their faces too. The longer I stay in here, the more I'm beginning to wonder if I really did do it."

I leaned forward. "Ralph, I'll never be able to make anybody understand if I can't explain it to my own client, so listen to me carefully. I don't care whether

74

you did it or not. Whether you're the Bay Ripper or Jack the Ripper is no concern of mine. I'm going to work as hard as I can to defend you. If lawyers had to convince themselves of their client's innocence before taking their cases, there wouldn't be many trials."

Ralph looked up from his slump. "But I want you to believe that I'm innocent, Mr. Armstrong. I know I lied to you about screwing that girl, but she's the only one, and I never killed anybody. Never. Hansen beat that confession out of me. You've got to get them to throw it out."

"I'm going to try, Ralph, but it's just your word against Hansen's. Besides, if they have the evidence Casey says they have, they don't even need the confession. But we won't know for sure until we see the indictment. They'll have to arraign you by tomorrow or ask for a postponement so we'll know pretty soon. Today, let's go over the story one more time."

I took out my notepad and led Ralph through yet another detailed account of his arrest and interrogation by Hansen. If Ralph's version of the events that evening was true, I had a chance to get the indictment quashed. Remote, but a chance, nevertheless, and Ralph desperately needed a chance. After a period of getting the same answers to the same questions, I folded up my papers and told him I would visit him again tomorrow. I had arranged to have an answering service pick up my telephone calls, so I assured him he could reach me night or day.

Back outside, I breathed the fresh air with relief. Ever since I had won out over my own legal difficulties, I had never left any jail without pausing to be thankful that I was free to come and go as I pleased. I considered calling Pell again, but since it was already past ten I went directly to the Fairmount Hotel.

"Any messages for Pell?" I asked the desk clerk. When he found none in Box 1104, I knew where to go. A man, probably over forty but with the thin body and angular good looks of a male model, answered my knock.

"Mr. Pell?"

"Yes." He was still dressed in pajamas and a robe.

"I'm David Armstrong. Ralph Rodriguez's attorney."

"Oh, yes, Inspector Casey did say you would be coming, but I expected you to call first. I'd prefer to have my own attorney present."

"I'm not a cop," I said, "so I don't think you'll need a lawyer, and I did call earlier, but you didn't want to be disturbed until after ten." I glanced at my watch. "It's after ten."

Pell stepped aside to let me into the room and pointed to a table containing orange juice, bacon and eggs, coffee, and a single red rose in a vase. "I was just having breakfast. Can I order something up for you?"

I told him no thanks and sat down on a couch while he finished his breakfast. Between bites, Pell asked me what it was exactly that I wanted to know.

I wondered myself. Casey had done a good job of convincing me, but I could not see how the same reasoning would have persuaded Pell.

Answering myself aloud, I said, "I want to know why you changed your mind, Mr. Pell. On Saturday you wanted Hansen's badge, and now Casey tells me you're willing to drop the whole thing. Why?"

Pell finished his toast and pushed the rest of the food away from him. "I was upset on Saturday, Mr. Armstrong. And irrational. You see, my family has just

76

as much money as Wendy's, but we're not so well
known. And that's the way we want to keep it. That's
why I've agreed to let Inspector Casey handle the whole
thing within the department. If you can avoid bringing
this matter out in open court, I would sincerely appreciate it."

"What matter? I can't see how Hansen's behavior
that night has anything to do with your family or you. I
think you'd better let me know what's going on."

"I'd like more assurance from you before . . ."

I interrupted him. "Mr. Pell, I'm representing a man
facing eight counts of murder, and the only assurance I
can give you is that I will explore every aspect of this
case on his behalf. I'm not going to try to bluff you. I'm a
new lawyer with no resources to hire a private inves-
tigator, but I'll get to the bottom of this story if I have to.
I don't want to cause you any more suffering, but if I
think your testimony will help Rodriguez, I'll subpoena
you. If I find out the whole thing's not pertinent, I'll
forget about it. I'm sorry, but those are my only options.
The choice is strictly up to you."

Pell looked away from me as he said, "I'm sure Inspector Casey has told you everything, but I'll go over it
again if you insist." He stood up and walked over to a
window that overlooked Nob Hill and the bay. "Wendy
called me here the night she was murdered. To taunt
me with the fact that she and Hansen had made love. I
went over to her aunt's house and threatened to report
Hansen to his superiors, and he took me to a neighborhood bar to talk me out of it. After a few drinks I
calmed down a little, and he brought me back to the
hotel. But when he called a couple of hours later to tell
me Wendy was dead, I lost control. Completely. I went

down to the Hall of Justice, but I couldn't get any satisfaction, and the next morning I filed a formal complaint. However, after discussing it with Inspector Casey, my attorneys and I decided it would be in our best interests to avoid publicity and allow the police to deal with Hansen in their own way."

"Several questions," I said. "How did you know she was at her aunt's house? Why hadn't you taken her home from the hearing? And why are you staying here instead of at your apartment?"

Pell walked away from the window and took a seat on the sofa across from me.

"She told me she was at her aunt's house," he said. "And I had been there on several occasions. As for the apartment, I moved out the night Wendy was raped. We'd gone to Perry's for dinner that evening, and she started coming on to one of the bartenders. We fought about it and I left, checking in here. It had happened before, so she knew where to reach me. When she called to tell me she had been raped, I assumed she and the bartender had made it together, and I hung up on her. But she was very upset and kept calling, begging me to come home. I suppose she would still be alive if I had."

Almost everything Pell was telling me I had heard from Casey, so I tried a different approach.

"Inspector Casey told me Hansen had made sexual advances to Wendy Horn, but now you're saying that she not only accepted them but bragged about it to you. And you were unconcerned and unbelieving of her rape story." I paused for a moment, deep in thought, then added, "I think the person both you and Casey are trying to protect is Wendy Horn. You don't care about yourself or your family or Hansen. You care about Wendy's reputation, and Casey doesn't want a promiscuous murder victim in the trial. Isn't that right?"

Pell laughed an unfunny laugh. "Promiscuous is hardly the word, Mr. Armstrong. Wendy was a very, very, very friendly girl."

I nodded and waited him out.

"I had known her all my life, so I don't know why her behavior continued to upset me. We grew up two houses apart in a suburb of Minneapolis. I was several years older, but we started sleeping together when she was only fourteen. One summer I came home from college and found her and my father in our sauna together, completely naked. She was giving him a massage. My father swore nothing else happened, but I broke up with Wendy then and didn't see her again until we were both in New York several years later. We started living together on Gramercy Park and tried to make it work. Neither of us had to earn a living or worry about anything else on earth except each other, but we argued constantly. My jealousy created a hell for me. I was in a world that I couldn't change, like a sailor with incurable seasickness. Wendy was, as you know, a remarkably beautiful girl, and it was her whole existence. Most women play many different roles. They are workers, friends, lovers, at different times with different people. But Wendy wasn't like that. No matter what she was doing, what she wore or where she was, men looked at her the same way, and she knew it. She once told me that she actually considered it selfish not to share her beauty. I'll never forget the going-away party we gave when we decided to move out here. There must have been a hundred people in the apartment. Couples, friends, relatives. Wendy took me aside at one point and confessed that she had been to bed at least once with every man in the room. Every one of them. And it was never any different out here."

I did not know what else to say, so I got up and said, "Thanks, Mr. Pell. I appreciate your telling me this."

Pell stood up also and asked, "What are you going to do? Will you use it at the trial?"

"No, I don't think so. I really don't think any of this has anything to do with Ralph Rodriguez."

We thanked each other again and I left. I paused in the lobby to telephone Casey, but he was not in, so I left a message and headed back to Sausalito. The message simply said that I agreed that no purpose would be served by a public disclosure of the Pell situation.

It was about noon when I got home. I made a peanut butter and jelly sandwich, washed it down with beer, and telephoned the answering service. I had already received three messages. One from a James Lambert, one from Abe, and one from Jennifer. Jennifer was in class and could not call back, but the message instructed me to watch a television channel for news specials. Abe wanted me to meet him at an address on Bush Street at three o'clock.

I turned on the TV, but a game show was in progress, so I lowered the volume and dialed Lambert's number. A voice announced, "Office of the Chief Assistant District Attorney." I identified myself, and Lambert came on the line.

"Mr. Armstrong, I understand you're the counsel in the Rodriguez case. We'd like to arraign him first thing tomorrow morning. Can you be there?"

I assured him I could, and he told me to be in Judge Peter J. Choy's courtroom at ten Tuesday. "By the way," he added, "I don't know if you've been informed yet, but the Grand Jury just returned a true bill of indictment against Rodriguez for eight first-degrees."

I thanked him, turned up the TV volume so that I could hear the news when it came on, and went to work at my desk. My law library was still small, but it was quite comprehensive with respect to criminal procedure, and I had already formed the basic outline of my motion when my attention was captured by Carolyn Mackay's voice.

Returning to the living room, I stood in front of the TV set. Carolyn Mackay was a past-middle-aged local reporter who had received a lot of publicity from exposés. She was standing on the steps of the Hall of Justice with a microphone in her hand.

"For the past six months this city has lived in terror. Arlene Harrington, Diane Willdorf, Janet Wickes, Barbara Schur, Karen Hall, JoAnne Paulsen, Wilma Owens, and Wendy Horn were all young and beautiful, and now all are dead. Each of them was raped and brutally mutilated and killed by a man the police say worked in the very office set up by the city to help them—the Rape Bureau of the Health Department. Ralph Rodriguez, a Mission Street Chicano with a wife and family, will be brought before Superior Court Judge Peter J. Choy tomorrow morning to answer charges that he murdered all these young women; that he is, in fact, the Bay Ripper. This reporter will be here tomorrow, and we will cover the trial from beginning to end, through all the delays and tactics that are common in such cases, until justice is done, one way or the other. And tonight, on the six o'clock edition, we will interview the arresting officer, Inspector James Hansen of Homicide, whose efforts were responsible for solving these crimes. In another exclusive, it has come to our attention that the defense attorney for Rodriguez is a David Armstrong of Sausalito, who was admitted to the Bar only last week after receiving a diploma from a mail-order school and who is himself an ex-felon with a record in New York. What is concerning officials in the Hall of Justice right this minute is whether Armstrong's background and lack of experience may leave this trial open to later appeals that Rodriguez did not receive competent counsel. We will explore this and other details of this bizarre and history-making trial tonight and in our continuing special reports. This is Carolyn Mackay."

I almost broke the knob on the television set as I turned it off. I grabbed another beer from the refrigerator and went back to my desk. A quick research of the common law on libel and slander reinforced my memory. I could sue her. Accusing a person of being a criminal after that person had been pardoned was unquestioned defamation of character, and the courts had been harsh in their judgments against it. In my situation it was even a clearer violation, since the record had been expunged as if it had never happened. I planned to sue Carolyn Mackay and Inspector Hansen for millions, absolutely millions of dollars.

Sitting there, pondering my action, listening to the tide splash against the rocks outside my window, I realized I had tears in my eyes, and the realization halted me. Tears were anger, Abe always said. And when you're angry you act compulsively and unconsciously. I could imagine what Abe would say to me. I would explain everything I felt, and he would grin that grin that encompassed both patience and understanding and say, "What's going on here, David? What's really happening?" Then he would tell me how proud he was of Jennifer and me because of what we had done with our relationship, how we continued to overcome our destructive motivations. "When I think back to what you were when I first met you, David, and see what you've become today, I'm actually awed. You've achieved something enormous. So don't be tricked into a battle with these people. You're fighting City Hall here, and you can't win. If you spit in their soup, they'll make you eat it. They're all convinced that what they're doing is right and they're just protecting their territory. Everybody does. So do you. Let them attack you; let them do whatever they want. All you really care about is defending your client. And you can't help him if you're trying to cover yourself. You need all your energy and talent for him. So don't get sidetracked, David, the way you used to. Leave the windmills to Don Quixote." And he would grin yet again, the grin that said I knew he was right, and I would return the grin and embrace the little pixie because he was right and because I loved him and because he always helped me so much.

When I got up and telephoned the most famous attorney in San Francisco, I had no idea whether he would even talk to me, but I described myself as a fellow lawyer and was surprised when a voice answered, "Benjamin Burger here."

After telling him I was the defense counsel in the Bay Ripper case and explaining about the Mackay slander, I said, "I was all prepared to sue her myself when I had a talk with my father-in-law, who reminded me of something I had forgotten—that a lawyer representing himself has a fool for a client. So, if you think I have a case,

Mr. Burger, I would consider it an honor if you would take it on a contingency basis. On any percentage you see fit."

"When can you come to my office?"

"After the arraignment tomorrow morning. Probably around twelve or twelve-thirty."

"Fine. Plan to have lunch with me here. I'll have it sent in. See you tomorrow."

I felt a lot better, and since it was still over an hour and a half before I had to meet Abe, I decided to prepare dinner. After putting on a half-dozen potatoes to boil, I went into town for the rest of my requirements. I bought a pound of cooked and cleaned fresh shrimp at the fish market, picked up a loaf of sourdough bread at the bakery, and stopped at the corner store for lettuce and tomatoes and a dozen yellow roses.

Back in the apartment, I placed the roses in a vase on our dining table and waited for the potatoes to cook. When they were ready, I skinned and sliced them while they were still hot, and with the addition of mayonnaise and chopped onion, my pure New York style potato salad was complete. Next I hollowed out three tomatoes, sculpted the edges into hills and valleys, and stuffed them with the shrimp. Then I put each of the tomatoes on a bed of washed lettuce, surrounded them with asparagus tips, olives, and pickles, and stored them in the refrigerator. Dinner was ready, and I had plenty of time to meet Abe.

The houses on Bush Street were all very old, but in most cases their intricately designed Victorian façades were flawlessly maintained. I saw Abe's car in front of the address he had given me. The house was two-storied, blue with white trim, and several of the windows were of stained glass. Abe was standing on the doorstep talking to Doctor Paley. I parked my car and walked up to the house.

"You know my son-in-law, I believe," Abe said.

"Yes, we met in court." Doctor Paley nodded to me. "What can I do for you, Mr. Armstrong?"

"I'm sorry to disturb you at home," I said, still not sure why Abe had arranged for us to meet her here instead of at the Rape Bureau. "I'd just like to ask you a few questions about Ralph, and then we'll be on our way."

"Do I have to answer them? Mr. Davidson has already asked quite enough questions to suit me."

"You can answer them here or you can answer them in court," I stated bluntly. "I know this must be disturbing to you, but imagine how upsetting it is for Ralph."

"Very well." She opened the front door and led us inside the house through a paneled dark hallway into what would normally have been used as a living room. What I saw, however, looked and smelled more like a hospital ward. A very old and frail man was propped up in an adjustable bed in the center of the room watching a television set. The volume on the set must have been turned up to absolute maximum.

Doctor Paley walked over to the bed and shouted, "YOU'LL HAVE TO USE THE EAR PLUG, FATHER. I WANT TO TALK TO SOMEONE."

She placed a plug in the old man's ear, then connected the other end to the television set, instantly cutting off the outside speaker. A tube was attached to the man's arm, and another extended out from beneath the sheets. Doctor Paley checked both of them, tucked the sheets in tightly, and returned to Abe and me.

"He watches television day and night," she ex-

85

plained. "The plug hurts his ear after a while, so I usually just let him keep it on full blast."

She motioned us to a couch and took a chair facing us. Crossing her arms and legs, she asked, "Now, what was it you wanted to know?"

I reached for my briefcase and took out a yellow pad. I considered momentarily also taking out my pipe and tobacco pouch, but the sterile atmosphere of the room and the absence of ashtrays discouraged me from smoking.

"How long have you known Ralph?" I asked.

"Since he was assigned to the Bureau. December of last year."

"Do you know him well? Have you ever spent any time with him away from work?"

"Absolutely not," she said quickly, answering my second question first. "I only speak to him within the framework of my duties at the Bureau. I haven't the slightest idea what kind of person he is, and I have no control over the people sent to work for me."

"What actually did he do at the Rape Bureau, Doctor?"

"He kept records, maintained the supplies, and performed simple lab tests. His title was Technical Assistant."

"I'm sure you're aware that the police have found out that all the Bay Ripper's victims had previously reported a rape to the Bureau. Obviously Ralph had access to the files, but I don't understand why you or someone else there didn't make a connection sooner."

"I explained all that to Inspector Casey, Mr. Armstrong. It's true what you say, but Ralph had very little contact with the patients. The whole idea of the

Bureau was to have a sympathetic woman receive the complaints. And the volunteer women who took the calls got hundreds every day. They were just names and voices to them and soon forgotten. As for me, I work night and day examining those girls. Rapists don't commit their crimes at convenient times, I'm afraid."

"I believe Inspector Casey said you never read newspapers?" Abe asked.

"That's correct, Mr. Davidson. I'd never even heard of the Bay Ripper until Wendy Horn was murdered. Between my job and caring for my father, I have no time for anything else. Now they've closed the Bureau, and all my work has been for nothing. I'll . . ."

She interrupted her sentence in response to an unintelligible sound from her father, then went over to the bed and took a pan from beneath his body, replacing it with a clean one from a nearby stand. After taking the first pan into the bathroom, she returned to the living room.

"I hope those are all the questions you had, Mr. Armstrong?"

Abe and I rose. When we had first come in, I noticed a science-fiction serial on the TV, and now I saw that it was an animated program for children. The old man seemed unaware of any reality beyond the screen he was watching.

"How old is your father, Doctor Paley?"

"Quite old, Mr. Armstrong," she said, escorting us to the front door, her eyes flashing. "I really must insist. No more questions." It was the same cold expression I had seen earlier in the courtroom, and I wondered if life as a rape specialist was responsible for it.

Outside, Abe and I both looked back at the house for

a moment before arranging to meet at the apartment after I picked up Jennifer.

I took the car up California and through the park to Irving. Jennifer was waiting for me outside the school, and I felt the tension the moment she entered the car.

"What's wrong?" I asked.

She slammed the door behind her and said, "What's wrong? Didn't you get my message? Everybody in the school has seen that news special."

She was very agitated, but I kept calm. The only time Jennifer and I ever really argued was when we were both angry at the same time. Usually, even though it took a great deal of effort, one of us was able to hold the balance. Jennifer had certainly had her share of the part, so I knew it was my turn today.

I said, "Yes, I saw the newscast."

"What did you do about it?"

Consciously keeping an even tone, I said, "It's a long story, darling. Why don't we wait until we get home, and I'll tell you and Abe together."

"Oh, David, it was terrible. All day long everybody was just looking at me. The students and everybody. I was able to talk to a couple of my friends at lunch, but it's just been a horrible day. I wish you'd never taken this case. I wish you'd never met Ralph Rodriguez."

She bit her lip to keep from crying, but she was not totally successful, and I pretended not to notice as we drove on toward the bridge. We didn't say any more until we got back to the apartment.

Abe was seated on the terrace, sipping a scotch.

"Couldn't wait," he yelled, waving us out.

Jennifer noticed the yellow roses as soon as we en-

tered the apartment. She moved closer to me, squeez-
ing my hand. "I'm all right," she whispered, and I kissed
her on top of the head as we joined Abe.

After I had prepared a Dubonnet for Jennifer and a
scotch for myself, I loosened my tie, took out my pipe
and tobacco and said, "Okay, Abe. You first."

Abe paused to put on his glasses, then took a notepad
out of his shirt pocket. "I took Jennifer to school, and
then I started looking for Rodriguez's friends. I found
one—Juan Zavala—at home. He doesn't have a job. He
said he remembered leaving the courthouse after the
hearing about noon and going with you and Jennifer
and Ralph and his family and two other friends to a
Mexican restaurant. He doesn't know exactly how long
he was there, but he recalls you two leaving before
everybody else. He and Rodriguez went with the others
to a place called Mission Rock to play pool and drink
beer. He's sure he was home before eleven that night."

"Will he testify if we need him?"

"Oh, sure. He's very cooperative. He's the one who
sat in for Rodriguez at the hearing." Abe checked his
notes again and said, "Mercado's a truck driver on a
three-day haul, so I couldn't talk to him, but I found
Ruiz at the Greyhound maintenance yard on Seventh.
He's a bus washer. His story confirms Rodriguez's also,
and he'll be glad to testify."

"Did you believe these guys, Dad?" Jennifer asked.

"Oh, I suppose so, honey. But how can you tell? I
asked Zavala if he was lying to me, and he said, 'No, sir,
I don't lie.' Then I asked him if he would lie for Rodriguez if he had to, and he said, 'Sure.' "

"Hold on a minute," I said. Jennifer was still nursing

her drink, but Abe and I needed refills. While I was in the kitchen I heard Abe describing Doctor Paley's house to Jennifer.

"Why did you want to meet there, anyway?" I asked, returning with the drinks.

"Well, the Greyhound facility is only a few blocks from the Hall of Justice, so I went to the Rape Bureau, but it's closed up. A sign refers all visitors to the police department. I looked up her name in the directory and called her, told her who I was and that we wanted to talk to her. I got there a few minutes before you did and found out that she and her father have been living in that house since she entered medical school at Berkeley. Her father was a doctor in Santa Rosa but retired at about that same time. Apparently he and her mother are separated or divorced, but I couldn't pin her down. She has one younger sister, and that's all I could find out. She didn't care for my questions."

"What do you make of that?" I asked.

Abe grinned. "Not much. A lot of people don't care for my questions." He took a drink of his scotch and said, "What about you? How did it go with Mr. Pell?"

I told him and Jennifer about my discussion with Pell, about the District Attorney's call, and then about the Carolyn Mackay news special revealing my police record.

"What was your reaction?" Abe asked.

"Explosive at first. I tore around this apartment in a rage, and in about fifteen minutes I had sued everybody concerned for something like a billion dollars."

"And?"

"And then I had a long talk with you, Abe. You told

90

me how proud you were of Jennifer and me because we had learned to channel our emotions constructively. You reminded me about false pride; you told me to keep my head, not be distracted by the enemy, and to remember that I had only one task—to defend Ralph Rodriguez." I raised my glass and added, "Thanks."

"That's brilliant," Abe said. "I couldn't have said it better if I had been here." The grin that I had expected appeared.

I continued, "So after our talk I called Benjamin Burger and asked him to handle the lawsuit for me. I'm having lunch with him tomorrow in his offices."

"Benjamin Burger!" Abe exclaimed. Jennifer got up suddenly and went into our bedroom. Abe and I glanced at each other before I followed her.

She was sitting on the edge of our bed, crying. I put my arm around her as she said, "I'm sorry I was so bitchy in the car, David. I didn't mean what I said about wishing you had never taken the case. I'm proud of what you're doing, and I've never, ever been ashamed of you. That's why I was so mad. I wanted to tell all those people pitying me that *I* didn't share their concern, that *I* didn't care. Do you understand?"

I held her close. "I certainly do, darling, but I still wish you hadn't had to go through that."

Jennifer sat up straight and wiped the tears from her eyes. "Well, I'm up to it, David, and you'd better be also. We can't deliberately set our course for a storm and expect to have a relaxed and placid trip."

I had to agree, and we resealed our pact with a kiss. I returned to the terrace while she freshened up.

"Is she all right?" Abe asked.

91

I sat back down and reclaimed my drink. "Jennifer Davidson Armstrong is just fine, thank you. In fact, she couldn't be better."

Jennifer, wearing a loose-fitting blue lounging gown, rejoined us shortly. "All right, guys. Let's have some dinner. What'll it be?"

"Dinner is all ready," I announced and led them to the table. I went into the kitchen and sliced the bread, opened a bottle of chilled white wine and took the plates out of the refrigerator. I sprinkled parsley over each of the stuffed tomatoes before passing them over the counter, receiving only groans of pleasure in response.

During the meal we continued to discuss the case. Abe said, "We've talked to everybody we had to, David, so I'm going back to Bodega Bay after dinner. Have you decided on your tactics yet? How are you going to defend this thing?"

"Everything centers around Inspector Hansen. The discovery of the body, the arrest, the evidence, the confession, everything. If the jury believes him, Ralph is dead. I'm going to have to attack him on the witness stand and hope I can crack his story, maybe even get it thrown out at the preliminary hearing. It's really the only chance we've got."

"Do you think you can do that?" Jennifer asked.

"I don't know. We'll just have to see. Attorneys do it all the time on television."

9

I awakened before dawn the next morning and went for a stroll along the rocky beach the bay gave us at low tide. Then I made coffee, trimmed my beard, showered, and changed suits twice before finally selecting the camel-colored one that Jennifer had bought at Gene Hiller's in town for my last birthday. With flared pants, checkered vest and wide lapels, it might have been considered too flashy for court, but it was my best suit, and I knew the television reporters would be at the courthouse.

When I left for town to take the early ferry, Jennifer was still sleeping. I walked down the hill, took a shortcut past the Valhalla Inn, owned by a onetime madam, and came out on Bridgeway. It was an absolutely clear morning, with a mild breeze coming off the water, and

93

as always the walk made me conscious of how fortunate I was to live in such a place.

Although the ferry would be filled with tourists later in the afternoon, the early-morning passengers were regular commuters. I stood on the front deck, with the wind and the spray hitting me in the face, and watched the little fishing boats tug out to sea in a line, their dirty, ocean-stained bows appearing freshly painted as they glistened against the unfolding day and the white city beyond. It seemed to me a magical way to go to work, but most of the people on board were hunched over their newspapers and coffee, as oblivious to their surroundings as riders on a subway. When the boat docked at the Embarcadero, I took a cab to the Hall of Justice.

It was still early when I got there. Only a few people were in the building, and I could smell the disinfectant on the recently mopped floors. As I walked down the long corridor toward Judge Choy's court, the sound of my heels on the marble floor made me aware of the solitary task ahead of me. I sat down on one of the benches with a cup of vending-machine coffee and waited.

By ten o'clock the hallway was crowded, and the people became a flood that rushed toward the opening courtroom doors. I had been looking for Ralph's mother and wife, but I didn't see them, so I pushed my way inside and went directly to the counsel table. A man I assumed to be Lambert was already seated at the table to my right, and we nodded cordially to each other.

Rodriguez was brought in, dressed in the same blue suit he had worn at the rape trial. A deputy placed him in a chair next to me and then remained standing behind us at the railing. Ralph looked scared, and I hoped the empathy I felt for him did not look like fear also.

When the bailiffs finally closed the doors, there was not an empty seat in the courtroom. Judge Choy entered, motioned for everyone to be reseated, and began the proceedings.

"The matter before the court is case number 784901, the People of the State of California, plaintiff, versus Ralph Rodriguez, defendant. The defendant is represented by David Armstrong. Are you, sir, Mr. Armstrong?"

"I am, your honor," I said, rising and placing my hand on Ralph's shoulder. "And this is my client, Mr. Rodriguez."

"I note that appearing for the People is Mr. James Lambert, Chief Assistant District Attorney."

Lambert stood also to acknowledge his presence, and Judge Choy said, "Very well, this morning the court will hear only pleadings. If either of you has any pretrial motions, we'll set a date for future hearings convenient to both parties. Mr. Armstrong?"

"Your honor, although I have not yet received a copy of the Grand Jury transcript, I waive a formal reading of the charges. The defendant pleads not guilty to all counts."

Lambert stood up and said, "We've already mailed a copy to Mr. Armstrong."

The judge nodded, and I continued: "We have prepared a motion for bail outlining all of the facts about Mr. Rodriguez, his family and his background, which includes no criminal record and a stable job history. But we also respectfully request that bail be granted in this case as a matter of law."

"What law, Mr. Armstrong?"

95

Amateur Hour

"As I understand it, your honor, bail can only be withheld when the proof of guilt is evident or the presumption thereof great."

"Yes?" The judge's expression was skeptical.

I knew I would not win the motion, but I had to see it through. "Well, in this case all the evidence is circumstantial, and I plan to contest most of its admissibility. We will attempt to show that the arresting officer, Inspector Hansen, has acted irresponsibly and even criminally by . . ."

Lambert was on his feet. "The People strenuously object to this police officer's being maligned in this manner. He is not on trial here."

The judge agreed. "Confine your comments to the bail issue, Mr. Armstrong."

"Your honor, my argument is simply that, since I plan to test the legality of all the evidence against my client, I feel there is enough doubt of his guilt to grant him bail now, and I so move."

Lambert tried to rebut but was interrupted by a voice from the spectator area.

"If it please the court, before the prosecutor speaks, I would also like to speak on behalf of the defendant's right to bail."

The man, whom I immediately recognized from pictures I had seen of him, was Carl Davis, a local attorney nationally famous for representing political radicals.

"Upon what basis do you ask to speak, Mr. Davis?" asked Judge Choy, who also realized who he was.

"*Ex parte*, your honor," Davis said as he came through the gate separating the court from the audience area. "My participation in this case is so recent that I have not yet had a chance to speak to the defendant or his counsel, but I'm happy to offer my services

96

on behalf of the Mexican-American Defense League, and I request to speak as someone who is not a party to the proceedings but who has an interest in it."

I was still looking at Ralph for an explanation, and wondering whether or not to object, when the judge spoke.

"This court is aware of your well-deserved reputation, Mr. Davis, and when the defendant formally petitions for your assistance at the defense table, you'll be welcome. But for today we shall continue without you."

Davis bowed and returned to his seat. I noticed for the first time that Anna and Mrs. Rodriguez were sitting with him, and I was beginning to get angry. Lambert was starting his argument against bail, but I heard only parts of it as I pondered the meaning of Davis's appearance.

When Lambert was finished, Judge Choy said, "I'll rule on the bail motion at a later hearing. Any other motions?"

I stood up again and said, "Yes, your honor, I've prepared briefs to suppress the evidence, including the confession. I'd also like to make a routine motion for discovery."

"All right. Why don't we meet again Thursday morning and hear those, if that's convenient?"

"That's fine for the People, your honor," Lambert replied, "but we'd like to raise the issue of a gag order from the bench. This case has already generated a tremendous amount of publicity, and my office is concerned about its effect on the trial. I'm sure Mr. Armstrong agrees with us."

The judge peered down at me and asked, "Mr. Armstrong?"

"My client has no desire to relinquish any of his

97

rights, your honor, including the right to a public trial."

"In that case, let's adjourn until next Thursday, gentlemen. You can leave your briefs with the clerk." Judge Choy stood up, ending the hearing.

I turned and told the deputy I wanted to talk to Ralph before he took him back to jail, and the deputy led us into a conference room next to the judge's chambers. Ralph's mother and wife came in behind us, followed by Carl Davis and two companions.

The deputy closed the door behind us, and Ralph's mother immediately went over to her son and embraced him.

I interrupted them to inquire whether Ralph had asked Davis to be in court.

"I told you Momma had gone to the League for help, Mr. Armstrong."

Davis stepped forward. "Maybe I can explain. Mrs. Rodriguez requested our assistance in getting her son out of jail. That's why we're here. I've been very busy and didn't have a chance to contact you beforehand. I'm sorry if I'm stepping on your toes."

"Mr. Davis, you're a famous lawyer, and I know I should be grateful for your offer, but I'm just not interested in partners." I turned back to Ralph and said, "I defended you successfully at the rape trial, Ralph, and I'll try to do the same thing here, although I've never tried to hide the seriousness of this case from you." I directed my attention to his mother next. "Mrs. Rodriguez, when I first spoke to you, I told you I didn't want any fee for that trial, and I don't expect any for this one, but I think you owe me the right to represent Ralph on my own. If you want Mr. Davis, I'll step out."

One of the young men accompanying Davis spoke

up. "You need organized help, mister. These California pigs are always framing Chicanos. They put Juan Corona and Inez Garcia away, and they'll do the same to Rodriguez unless we stop them."

I was controlling my temper, but it was difficult. "I'm not defending a Chicano, mister," I answered. "I'm defending Ralph Rodriguez. And as long as I have anything to do with it, nobody's going to turn this trial into a political platform. I have very little use for politicians of any kind, whether United States senators or street revolutionaries, especially in a courtroom."

Davis frowned at my remarks and threw open his arms. "I'm sorry, Mr. Rodriguez, but if your counsel objects to my participation, there's nothing I can do. Professional ethics prevents me."

We all waited while Ralph conversed in feverish Spanish with his mother. When they were finished, he announced, "My mother says to thank you, Mr. Davis, for your concern, but if Mr. Armstrong doesn't want you, we have no choice. My mother says he is a good man who stood by me, and I must stand by him."

Davis shrugged and motioned for his companions to follow him out of the room. He paused at the door.

"I heard about the stunt you pulled at the rape hearing, Armstrong. You were lucky you had a liberal judge. If you try that kind of thing with Peter Choy, you'll spend a good deal of your career in jail for contempt. Good luck, though."

After Davis had gone, I thanked Mrs. Rodriguez for her support and told Ralph I would visit him again before Thursday's hearing. Outside the room, I asked the deputy to let them have a few more minutes together before taking him back, then deposited my briefs on the clerk's table and went out into the hallway.

I was assaulted by microphones and floodlights. Lambert was facing one group of cameras, while Davis was being interviewed by some other reporters nearby.

"Hey," one of them yelled, "here's Rodriguez's attorney now. Let's get him."

I allowed myself to be positioned next to Davis as he was answering a question.

". . . and so the present counsel and I have just concluded a conference with the defendant and his family, and it has been decided that I will not assist at this time."

"At any time," I heard myself say.

"Why don't you want Davis's help?" a reporter asked, and Davis answered for me.

"I'm afraid Mr. Armstrong's political consciousness is not developed enough for him to see the ramifications of this trial. But if lawyers always agreed, there would never be any lawsuits, would there?"

The reporters around us were crowding closer, their microphones extended in front of them, their questioning voices crying out for recognition.

"Mr. Armstrong, Mr. Armstrong, aren't you concerned about trying this case alone, now that there are charges that you have a police record?"

I connected Carolyn Mackay's face with the voice and said, "You mean your charges, don't you, Miss Mackay? I'm telling you right here and now that I've never been convicted of any crime, and every time you repeat that statement you are compounding the slander."

"Are you saying that . . ."

"I've already said it," I continued. "Furthermore, I'm

'on my way right now to retain Benjamin Burger in a lawsuit against you, Miss Mackay, your television station, and Inspector James Hansen of the police department. Now, if you'll excuse me," I added, wading into the throng, "I'm already late for the appointment."

They quieted momentarily and reluctantly cleared a path for me, like pigeons getting out of the way at the very last moment.

A cab took me to the financial district and let me out in front of the Burger Building. With its velvet draperies, rich wood paneling and Gay Nineties decor, the building was a reminder of San Francisco's bawdy past and served as a tourist attraction as well as an office. All of the offices were visible from the street, Burger's prominently, and passersby were continually peering in, trying to get a glimpse of the great man at work or to see one of the pretty secretaries he was noted for hiring. The girl who greeted me did not depart from that tradition, and I followed her short-skirted legs into Burger's office.

"Mr. Burger, this is Mr. Armstrong."

Burger was quite tall and portly, with gray hair befitting a man who had been practicing law for almost fifty years. He was dressed in a deep blue suit, a green cravat in place of a tie, and shining patent leather shoes. He thanked the girl and clasped my hand, patting me on the back as he led me to a leather chair facing his mammoth hardwood desk. The only furnishing in the room less than a century old was the television set, which he pointed to.

"You were on the twelve o'clock news just now. What happened with Carl Davis? Try to horn in on you?"

I nodded. Burger said, "Carl's a good man, but he gets

101

caught up with his clients and their causes. I'm a hired gun. I'll argue anybody's case if he's got the money. What about you?"

"I agree with you. That's why Mr. Davis is not coming into the case."

Half a dozen people were looking in the window at us from the sidewalk outside, and Burger walked over to pull the shades together.

"I don't mind their watching me work," he said, "but I like to eat in peace." He sat back down at his desk. "Those murders have got everybody keyed up, and it's going to be a sensational trial. How do you plan to defend your man?"

"I'm going to try to get the evidence thrown out at pretrial."

"Not a chance."

"Maybe, but there's no hope of an acquittal with the evidence they've got against him."

"I heard you got your degree from a correspondence school. What in the hell do you know about trying a murder case?"

"About the same as you did when you started, Mr. Burger. Did law school prepare you for your first murder trial?"

"I didn't go to law school."

"I know," I said. "I've got your autobiography at home. You read Blackstone for a few months, a circuit judge asked you four or five questions, and you were admitted to the Bar. So, now that we've established that we're both a couple of amateurs, will you take my lawsuit?"

Burger laughed heartily as he got up to answer the knock on his office door. "I have to. You've already told the world I'm representing you."

He opened the door to allow a waiter to wheel in our lunch, which was encased in gleaming stainless steel. The waiter removed the top, placed sautéed rex sole, potatoes and salad in front of us, and produced a bottle of chilled Chablis. After Burger had approved a sample of the wine, the waiter poured two glasses and left us.

"It's from Doros, next door," he offered. "I usually walk over for lunch, but I wanted to talk with you in private today." He tasted his fish before adding, "The first thing we have to do is figure out how you can win this murder trial. Then you'll be worth something. Right now, they've slandered a nobody."

I grinned at his frankness and asked, "Do you really think we have a slander case?"

"Oh, sure. I had our people check it out. Deferred sentence, full restitution, then dismissal of the charges. Anybody can find the original charges, but if they miss the dismissal they're slandering you. The TV station's lawyers will say there was no malicious intent, but I'll make so much noise they'll be glad to settle out of court."

"Do you need to know any more details? I have a complete file at home if it'll help."

Burger sipped some wine and said, "Hell, no. I don't want to hear another word about it. There's no need for you to have to keep dragging the story up. We've all done a few things we'd rather forget."

We ate the rest of our lunch in silence; then Burger wiped his mouth, tossed the cloth napkin onto the table and reached behind him to push a button on his desk telephone.

The waiter reappeared instantly and Burger waved him and the table out. I realized that the waiter had been standing outside the door the entire time. Burger

103

took out a cigar and offered me one also, but I pointed to my pipe, which I filled with tobacco.

After a ritual of rolling, cracking, smelling and clipping the cigar, Burger spoke from behind a wave of blue smoke.

"You know, Armstrong, some people think I'm a big criminal lawyer. The fact is, most of my cases have been torts, but I know enough to tell you that you're not going to win many murder cases at pretrial hearings. My first client was a black man accused of raping and murdering a little white girl, and I knew I didn't stand a chance with a jury, so I threw my man on the mercy of the court. The judge sentenced him to die three times." He paused, thinking about it, and added, "I considered it a moral victory that they actually hanged him only once."

I didn't know how to respond to that, and he continued, "What I'm telling you is that you're going to have to take your case to the jury. Don't worry about where you got your degree. The damn schools don't teach you a thing about being a courtroom lawyer anyway. They only devote a few hours the first year to the whole subject of criminal law. You'll have to learn it yourself. I've been doing it a long time and I still don't know all the answers." He flicked his cigar ashes and said, "Now, tell me what they've got on your client."

I told him everything that had happened—from the original rape trial to the present. I even told him about Pell and Wendy Horn. Waiting for his response, I felt like a student in front of a teacher.

"I think your boy's going to the gas chamber," Burger said flatly, "but I agree with you that your only chance is at pretrial. If that evidence goes to the jury, they'll convict." He sat back in his chair for a moment, enjoying his cigar. "You can try to break the cop's story, but it's very unlikely you'll succeed. Even if your guy is telling the truth, cops are used to lying in court. Your best bet is to find another witness to the arrest, an independent witness, somebody who lives in the Marina or who was there that night and saw what happened. If you can find somebody who actually saw the cop and Rodriguez drive into the Marina before the arrest, the cop's story might collapse. It's a real long shot, but you've got plenty of time before the trial. I'd even get some leaflets printed up, asking for information, and put them out all over the neighborhood."

He got up and went to the door. "Leave your name and telephone number with my girl, Armstrong, and I'll be in touch. Don't worry about the slander suit. I'll take care of it, and you concentrate on this trial. Whatever we get, we'll split down the middle."

He slapped me on the back and I was gone. The girl in the short skirt took down all the information and then wished me a nice day, smiling a spontaneous, wide-open smile. She was blond and tanned, and her dress concealed less of her body than it revealed. I wished her a happy day also and left.

I did not deceive myself that the girl had been flirting with me, but her friendliness added to the sense of well-being that engulfed me. I walked toward the ferry building, luxuriating in the midday sun and the natural beauty all around me. I had been a lawyer less than a week, and I had already won a rape case, had become counsel at a murder trial, and had met two of the most famous criminal attorneys in the country, one of whom was representing me. If this was the beginning of my long-delayed career, I wondered what the future held.

10

Wednesday was the last day I had to interview Ralph before the hearing, and I spent some time with him in the afternoon. The morning had been taken up following Burger's suggestion. A photocopy store had produced a leaflet for me, and I had distributed a copy to every house and apartment facing the Marina. I promised a small reward to anyone who had witnessed Ralph's arrest the night of the Horn murder, but when I called my answering service just before going into the Hall of Justice, there had been no response to the leaflets.

When Ralph was brought into the interview room at the jail, I handed him a pack of cigarettes and took out my own tobacco and my pipe and, without any pleasantries, began talking.

"The first thing I want to go over today is the hearing, Ralph. It'll be similar to the one we had at the rape trial, but there is almost no chance that the charges will be dropped, as they were then. The most we can hope for is that the judge will throw the confession out. There'll be a trial anyway, but if the confession is suppressed, we'll have a lot better chance with the jury. Do you have any questions about the hearing itself?"

Ralph shook his head, and I lighted my now-filled pipe before continuing.

"All right, the next thing I want to do is to go over your story from start to finish."

Ralph groaned in protest. "I've already told you everything, Mr. Armstrong. There's nothing . . ."

"Hold it. You don't have to do anything you don't want to do. The law says that everyone is entitled to the assistance of counsel, and that's why I'm here. But you're the one behind bars; you're the one on trial; and it's your life at stake; so you tell me what you want to do."

"Okay, man," he said resignedly, "you've made your point. Where do you want me to start?"

"Since you're so tired of the whole story, I'll just ask you about some areas that are bothering me. For instance, Hansen's going to testify that he found Wendy Horn's body, went outside the house, saw you across the street in your van and arrested you. You say Hansen actually came to your house, had you follow him in your van to the Marina, and arrested you there. Even though your stories are totally opposed, you both agree on one fact: Hansen never went inside your van, did he?"

"No. When we got to the Marina, he just pulled me out of the van and handcuffed me."

"Then how did Wendy Horn's panties get into your van?"

"I don't know. The other cops took the van downtown. Maybe they hid them there."

I shook my head. "I don't buy that. I can accept one overzealous detective trying to pad the evidence against you, but not everybody in the department. And how do you explain the list? Did Hansen go to the Rape Bureau, tear it out of the book, and then drop it beside Wendy Horn's body just to get you?"

"I can't think, Mr. Armstrong. You're getting me confused, like Hansen did that night."

I reached across the table and cupped Ralph's face in my hand, forcing him to look at me. "Well, you'd better think. You're going on trial for your life tomorrow, and there are parts of your story that I don't believe. Nobody else will, either."

I released his face and leaned back, waiting for him to light another cigarette before I continued. "Let's go on, and try not to feed me any crap. How about the night you broke into Wendy Horn's apartment? Why did you choose her?"

"The lights were off. She was on the ground floor. And it was an old house. The windows are easier in old houses."

"Okay. You broke in, but she woke up and surprised you. You threw a pillow over her face, raped her, and left. Weren't you afraid she'd report the rape to the Bureau and see you there?"

Ralph thought a moment before answering. "No, sir. I didn't think she got a good look at me, and like I explained, it wasn't really rape. She wanted it."

I slammed my fist on the table and almost shouted,

"It was rape, goddammit. Once and for all, you'd better know that. She didn't invite you there. You broke into her home, held her down and violated her body. That's rape, Ralph. And I'll bet you took her panties as a souvenir, didn't you? Admit it. I know you did."

Ralph did not answer.

"What did you do with them?" I persisted. "Show them off to your friends?"

He was still silent, and I continued, "So they all knew you'd raped her. You guys must have felt real big after the hearing. Did you decide to go one better and go back and gang-rape her? Is that what happened that night, Ralph? Did all of you go over there and rape her and then kill her?"

My voice had seemed very loud in the small room, and now that I was silent the quiet was exaggerated. It was some time before Ralph responded, and when he did, he spoke to the floor, unable to look at me.

"I did take her panties that night I broke into her apartment, Mr. Armstrong, but not the night she was killed. I had no way of knowing where she was."

"That list was cross-referenced with telephone numbers and addresses," I argued. "All you had to do was call the police. They would have given you the number where Hansen was. The rest would have been simple."

"But I didn't know Hansen was with her," Ralph said. He had regained some of his spunk and looked at me as he spoke. "He came to my house and took me to the Marina just like I told you. I swear it, Mr. Armstrong."

I believed him. Since he had been with me the whole time, in court and after, and since I had not known about Hansen's taking Wendy Horn home either, I had to believe him. And because I believed him, I realized suddenly that I had made a mistake in agreeing to

110

withhold information about Hansen's activities that night with Wendy Horn. And about Pell.

I stood up and said, "I don't know whether you've told me the truth about everything, Ralph, but you've convinced me that Hansen couldn't have arrested you the way he said he did. And that little crack in his story may be all I need to break him entirely. We'll see tomorrow in court."

I left him with the deputy and took the elevator to the Inspectors Bureau. Casey told the receptionist he was too busy to see me, but I insisted and was finally ushered back to his office.

He glanced up from a paper-strewn desk and said, "I don't know what's so urgent, Armstrong, but make it quick, please. I haven't even had time to take a piss today. Every damn reporter in the country, plus a dozen or so from overseas, is in here snooping around."

"I just came by to tell you in person that I'm going to have to go back on our agreement. I know you were sincere about your reasons for asking me not to drag Hansen and Pell into the trial, but I'm convinced Hansen is trying to frame my man, and I'm going to use everything I've got against him."

"Are you going into the sex angle too?"

"If I have to."

"Will you call Pell to the stand?"

"If I have to," I repeated.

"We all have to do what we have to do, Armstrong. But thanks for letting me know." He returned his attention to his desk as I left.

I had one more stop to make before picking up Jennifer. I drove to the China Basin looking for the Mission Rock Resort, which was a waterfront bar that also sold fuel and bait to fishing boats. I had torn a picture of

Ralph from the newspaper, and I took it inside to show it to the bartender. He had been on duty the night in question (he said he had not missed a Friday in over two years), but he could not identify the face. He saw a lot of Chicanos, but he didn't remember whether any had been in the bar that particular night. I thanked him and stayed for a beer and a game of pool until it was time to pick up Jennifer.

After a quick dinner of cheeseburgers and milk shakes at Bill's Place on Clement, Jennifer and I went straight to our apartment for an evening of pretrial preparation. While Jennifer sorted the Grand Jury transcript and other documents on the dining table, I telephoned my answering service.

"Burger was right," I said after hanging up the telephone. "There are no calls from the good citizens on the Marina."

"We didn't really expect any, so let's get to work. Everything you need is on the table." Jennifer positioned herself in a director's chair across the room from me, ready for the rehearsal.

I glanced through the papers on the table, made some notes on a pad, then approached Jennifer.

"All right, Inspector Hansen," I said, "let's begin with the evening of Wendy Horn's murder. Have you just testified that you were alone with Miss Horn for several hours until shortly before her death?"

"Yes."

"You testified that you left Miss Horn for a couple of hours and then returned to find her body. Is that correct, Inspector?"

"Yes."

"And isn't it true, Inspector, that you had intercourse with Miss Horn earlier and were afraid to report the murder immediately; that you concocted a scheme to trick the defendant, Rodriguez, into coming to the scene of the crime, knowing full well that he had been charged with raping the victim and would come under suspicion of murdering her? Isn't that true, Inspector Hansen?"

Jennifer frowned and asked, "Can you really ask me all that, David?"

I shook my head. "No, you're right. Those questions are outrageously leading. I was mostly just thinking out loud."

"Well, let's do it right. Start at the beginning and make me tell the whole story. And don't ask me anything that would be objected to."

She was right, and I returned to the table. Looking through the mass of material, I realized that if I was going to break Hansen it would probably be upon some seemingly minor point. If I focused my cross-examination on the sensational parts of his testimony, he would obviously be prepared for me. I decided to test him on even the smallest, most inconsequential facts and began again, using the Grand Jury transcript as a source.

It was a tedious procedure, but it succeeded spectacularly. After an hour of conspicuously terse replies to ostensibly innocent questions, our mock trial produced a situation in which Jennifer, as Hansen, had to lie. He had to lie in open court or expose himself as the architect of a frame-up. He had no other choices. Jennifer and I were ecstatic. Even if Hansen was telling the truth about everything else that happened the night of Wendy Horn's murder, one part of his story was so patently false that it could destroy his entire testimony.

113

11

Jennifer arranged for another teacher to handle her classes Thursday so that she could accompany me to court, and we went to the Hall of Justice together. Although we were half an hour early, the hallway into Judge Choy's courtroom was already filled with reporters and spectators. Guide ropes had been set up, creating a long line, but I was glad to see Ralph's wife and mother near the entrance. We waved to them as the deputy guarding the door allowed us to go in, and I made sure to save seats for them next to Jennifer.

When the courtroom was opened, Ralph's mother told us she had been waiting for hours after coming very early to bring Ralph clean underwear and a pressed shirt. I tried to reassure her about everything, and she looked up into my eyes with such a combination of fear

115

and hope that I spontaneously put my arms around her and hugged her to me. For a moment I wondered if I had been too familiar, but she responded by embracing me also, and I saw tears in her eyes. I reached out to include Ralph's wife, but a bailiff was shouting for everyone to be seated, and I hurried to my table.

Lambert and his assistant were already at the table to my right. Several law books, with yellow markers protruding from the pages, were stacked on the table. Lambert was obviously prepared to contest my motions. Casey and three other men sat in armchairs that had been placed just inside the railing behind Lambert's table, but I did not see Hansen in the courtroom.

Ralph was brought in, wearing his blue suit, and I whispered a quick greeting to him as the bailiff commanded us to rise for the judge.

Judge Choy motioned everyone back down and then announced that he had made his decision on two motions. He denied our request for bail, and he refused Lambert's plea for a gag order.

"However," he said, "I warn all parties to this action to limit their public comments to matters already in the record. Any questions, gentlemen?"

Neither of us had any, and the judge went on, "This court will now hear testimony on the defendant's motion to suppress a confession made by him which he contends was obtained in violation of his constitutional rights."

Lambert nodded and called his first witness. Doctor Banks testified that he worked as a volunteer physician for the sheriff's department, that he was on call the day following Ralph's arrest, and that he had examined Ralph in his cell without finding any indication of a beating or maltreatment of any kind. In his opinion, the cut and the inflammation in Ralph's finger could have been caused by almost anything, could even have been self-inflicted. Lambert introduced a photograph showing a naked Ralph in front, rear, and side poses. Doctor Banks identified the picture, said that he was the photographer, and pointed out that there were no visible wounds or bruises.

I did not ask the doctor any questions, and Lambert called Inspector Hansen to the stand.

After establishing that Hansen was a veteran police officer with a fine record, numerous citations, and no verified complaints, Lambert began to lead him slowly into his declaration. He offered into evidence the reports of the arrest and interrogation as well as Ralph's confession and questioned Hansen on every detail. My first impression was that Lambert was dull and plodding, but I soon realized what he was doing. By eliciting the facts so routinely, and in such abundance, he would prove their authenticity beyond doubt. I was also impressed by the way he cleared up inconsistencies, depriving me of the opportunity to dramatize them later.

"And after you found the list next to the dead girl's body, Inspector, what did you do next?"

"I went outside to look around. She hadn't been dead long. That's when I saw the defendant's van parked across the street from the house. I put two and two together and arrested him."

"What do you mean, 'put two and two together'?"

"Well, the girl had accused him of raping her a few days earlier, and . . ."

I jumped to my feet. "Your honor, those charges were dismissed, and I object to any reference to them."

117

"I'm merely trying to establish a foundation," Lambert argued.

"I'll allow it," Judge Choy ruled. "There's no jury present, and it relates to the witness's frame of mind."

Hansen continued: "As I was saying, I had booked him earlier in the week for raping the girl, and we had just left the hearing that day, so his identity was fresh in my mind. I thought of him the minute I found the list from the Health Department, and the first thing I see when I walk out is his van. I asked him what he was doing there, but he refused to say anything. I warned him of his rights, arrested him and searched him. I called for assistance, and when the boys arrived, we took him and his van downtown."

"Did you search the vehicle, and did you discover any evidence?"

"I didn't personally search the van, no, sir. I was busy interrogating the suspect. But Sergeant Kubik did, and he found a pair of silk panties with the initials WH embroidered on them."

I started to object, but Lambert waved me off and said, "Don't testify about Sergeant Kubik, Inspector. Just tell me about any evidence you personally uncovered. What about the list ostensibly taken from the Health Department? Did you take steps to determine that it was actually torn from a directory in that office?"

"Yes, sir. From the defendant's office. One of the first things I did when I got back to the Hall of Justice was to go downstairs to the Rape Bureau. The list matched up exactly with a page torn from the Bureau's directory."

"I see. And Sergeant Kubik found the panties soon after. But you still didn't know that all eight of the murder victims had a connection with the Rape Bureau, did you?"

118

"No, I didn't find that out till the next day when I went through their files."

"How did you get the defendant to confess, Inspector?"

"Normal procedure, sir. I just kept asking him what he was doing at the scene of the murder and how he came to have the dead girl's panties in his van until he eventually admitted it."

"Inspector Hansen, did you or anyone else, to your knowledge, ever strike, threaten or abuse the defendant in any way, or were any tricks used against him?"

Hansen shook his head and reiterated the absolutely perfect manner in which he had conducted himself and swore that he had warned Ralph of his right to remain silent and to have an attorney present.

"And did the defendant voluntarily sign his confession, which contained these warnings and his waiver of them, and was the confession properly dated and witnessed?"

When Hansen agreed with the statement, Lambert said that he had finished his direct examination.

The judge gave me a nod and I rose to face Hansen. He had stated a lot of facts, most of them just the way Jennifer had played his part the night before. Armed with the sure knowledge that he was lying, I advanced toward him.

"Inspector Hansen, I . . ." The words were barely out of my mouth when Lambert objected, and Judge Choy called us both to the bench.

The judge leaned forward and whispered, "Mr. Armstrong, I understand you're a new attorney, and you may not be aware of it, but the rule and custom in California courts is for counsel to remain behind the table when questioning witnesses."

Chagrined, I apologized and returned to my place, sighing with relief that he had been kind enough not to embarrass me in front of the entire courtroom and thinking that I had learned another lesson correspondence school had not taught me.

"Inspector Hansen," I continued from behind the table, "what were you doing in Wendy Horn's bedroom, anyway, when you discovered her body?"

Hansen immediately shifted his position in the chair, and Lambert and Casey stirred, but I knew there could be no objection. I was going right to the very area that Casey had hoped to avoid, but it was proper cross-examination, and there was nothing they could do about it.

"What do you mean?" Hansen asked.

"I mean exactly what I asked, Inspector. What were you doing there?"

"I had taken Miss Horn home after her appearance in court. She was upset and wanted protection."

"You were assigned to protect her?"

"No. I did it on my own. I was off duty."

"Why wasn't Miss Horn given official police protection if she was frightened?"

"There was no justification for it. Nobody had any idea then that there was a connection between rape victims and the Bay Ripper. But I felt sorry for her, so I took her home."

"What time did you leave the hearing with Miss Horn?"

"About noon, I guess."

"And what time did you leave her?"

"Eight o'clock."

"What were you doing with Wendy Horn from noon to eight, Inspector Hansen?"

120

Hansen shifted in his chair again. "Nothing. Just talking."

Everyone in the courtroom was quiet, and I let Hansen's answer lie in the stillness for several calculated seconds before continuing.

"Nothing, huh? Well, we'll come back to that. Let's go to another subject. You testified that you found Miss Horn's body at approximately ten-thirty but that you had left her at eight. Where were you for those two and a half hours?"

"With her boyfriend, Mr. Pell. We left her in the house and went out for some drinks."

"I plan to call Mr. Pell later, Inspector, to get his version of these events, but right now I'd like you to explain something for us. If, as you say, the only reason you took Wendy Horn home was because she was frightened, how could you have left her alone and unprotected?"

"I've already told you that nobody knew then about the link to the Bay Ripper. And as far as I knew, her location was a secret."

I started to ask my next question, but a deputy handed me a note which read:

Armstrong—Please hold off this line of questioning, at least until after the noon recess. Give me a chance to help you at lunch.

Casey

I glanced at Casey and nodded, then turned back to Hansen.

"Let's go into the arrest of the defendant, Inspector. You testified that you took Mr. Rodriguez into custody within a few minutes after finding the body at ten-thirty. What time did you obtain his confession?"

121

"I believe he signed it about three the next morning, but he had confessed an hour or so earlier. It took a while to get it typed up and everything."

"I see. You alone find the body. You alone apprehend the suspect. And you alone acquire the confession after about three hours of questioning in the middle of the night. Is that correct?"

"Just about."

"Don't you normally have more than one officer in the room during an interrogation? And isn't an assistant district attorney usually brought into these situations?"

"There is no normal. Each case is different. I'm assigned a partner, but, like I said, I was off duty. Since I'd arrested Rodriguez, he was my prisoner. I didn't need any help and I didn't ask for any. It was late and a weekend, and there weren't too many people around anyway, and I didn't see the sense in waking up an assistant D.A."

I checked off several questions listed on my yellow pad and saw that I had come to the crucial area, the part of his testimony where, if Jennifer and I were correct, he would have to lie or be exposed. I was ready to crush him, but I hesitated, wondering if I should wait. I checked my watch and decided to give him—and Casey—one last chance before declaring total war.

"With your honor's permission," I said, "I have only one other area I want to cover before lunch. I realize it's only a little past eleven, but I'd like to request an early recess. The witness has been on the stand for some time, and I still have a number of questions for the afternoon."

Lambert indicated that he had no objection, and Judge Choy nodded his head.

"Thank you, your honor. I'll just lay a foundation

before we break." I turned back to Hansen and asked, "Inspector, how long have you known the defendant?"

"I saw him for the first time the day I arrested him on the rape complaint."

"You had never seen him or noticed him, even though you both worked in the same building?"

"No. There must be hundreds of people working in this building."

"Have you ever been to the defendant's home?"

"No."

"Mr. Rodriguez claims that you arrested him at his home, not at the Marina. Are you sure you've never been to his home?"

"I never saw the man before a week or so ago, counselor, and I've never been to his house. I don't even know where he lives."

"Didn't you investigate him as a suspect in these murders after the rape charge?"

Hansen shook his head. "No more than any other sex offender. I checked him out, but he didn't have any priors. I didn't follow him or anything, if that's what you're getting at."

"So, you'd never seen Ralph Rodriguez before he was accused of rape, and you'd never been to his home or seen him at work, yet you recognized him immediately the night of the murder. Is that your testimony, Inspector?"

"That's right. I said before that his face was fresh in my mind because I had seen him at the hearing only a few hours before."

I told the judge I was finished for the time being, and he recessed court until two o'clock. A deputy took Ralph away, and Casey and I walked toward each other.

"Thanks," he said, "for holding back."

"It's just until after lunch," I said. "He's lying, and I can prove it."

Casey looked around and whispered, "Listen, I've still got the same concern about bringing those things out in open court, but I have my own doubts about some of his story now. You say you've got proof, so let's take him to lunch and lay it on him. If he admits anything, I'll do everything I can to help you."

I really was not sure what Casey was up to, but I made a quick decision and accepted.

"Good," he said, and walked over to Hansen, who was talking to Lambert. "Come on, Hansen, we're going to eat with Armstrong."

Hansen obviously had no desire to spend any time with me, but he was very deferential in the presence of the Chief Inspector.

"Let's go out the back way," Casey directed.

I turned around to see Jennifer and the two Rodriguez women waiting for me, but all I could do was wave before following Casey and Hansen into the room behind the court where the prisoners were held. We took the caged elevator down to the basement and came out of the building a block from the main entrance.

Casey suggested a restaurant which was some distance away but was not frequented by courtroom regulars, and we walked there in awkward silence. It was not until we were seated at a table and served drinks that Casey spoke.

"I didn't tell you this before, Hansen, but Mr. Armstrong has known about this mess with Wendy Horn for some time. He's been agreeable to keeping it out of the papers and out of court until now, and he still might be if we can talk a few things out here in private."

124

"What kind of things?" Hansen demanded, looking directly at me.

I looked right back at him and said, "What I want to talk about is that Ralph Rodriguez is sitting in a cell a few blocks away facing eight counts of homicide and the cop who gathered all the evidence against him is lying through his teeth."

Hansen glared across the table at me. "You son-of-a-bitch, I don't have to stay here and take that shit off you." He started to get up, but a glance from Casey kept him in his chair.

I took a drink of my scotch and said, in a lower tone of voice, "Look, Inspector Hansen, your sex life is none of my business. Wendy Horn was a beautiful girl and from what Pell told me a very seductive one, so I can hardly blame you. And I don't want to get into that in court unless I have to. But I'm convinced you framed my client to cover up your activities that night, and I'll use anything I've got until you admit it."

"You're talking through your hat," Hansen said.

"Mr. Armstrong says he has proof," Casey stated quietly.

"Yes, I do." The waiter came to take our order, but Casey waved him away and I turned to Hansen. "Your story is very pat, Inspector, but there are at least two gaps in it. And one of those gaps is so big that it tears down the whole thing."

I took some more scotch and continued. "The first gap is how Rodriguez knew where Wendy Horn was. I don't know how may people knew you were taking her to her aunt's house, but I certainly did not, and since Rodriguez was with me until we left the court and afterwards, he did not. So, even with the list, how did he find her?"

Hansen merely scowled and said, "If my grand-mother had balls she'd have been my grandfather. I don't deal in ifs. I have no idea how he got there, and I don't care. I saw him at the scene of a crime and I arrested him."

"All right, let's go to the second gap," I said. I was finally going to spend the currency Jennifer and I had worked so hard for. "There is no way you could have spotted Rodriguez in his van across the street that night."

"Yeah? Why not?"

"Because you had never seen his van before, Inspector Hansen."

His expression did not change, but he remained silent. Casey merely stared at both of us.

"That's the whole thing," I continued. "The big lie. You've just testified that you had never seen Rodriguez before the rape and that you'd never been to his home. So where in hell had you seen his van before that you could instantly recognize it on a dark street?"

"I don't have to answer that question. This is not a courtroom."

"You went to Rodriguez's home that night, didn't you, Inspector? And arrested him there, just like he said."

When Hansen did not reply, Casey said, "I'd like to know the answer to that question myself, Hansen."

"I've got to take a piss," Hansen said, quickly leaving the table.

Casey and I looked at each other for a moment; then Casey followed Hansen. I finished my drink, and when they had not returned for some time, I went to look for them. The door to the men's toilet was locked, but I could hear scuffling noises inside. I knocked several times, and Casey finally opened the door.

Hansen was on his knees in front of one of the stalls.

"Come on," Casey said, pulling me away. I told him we had to pay for the drinks, but he kept walking. "Forget it. Cops never pay."

We walked back to the Hall of Justice at a furious pace, Casey not answering my questions until we came to the rear of the building.

There, he caught his breath and said, "Look, Armstrong, I'll tell the D.A. what happened, but it's up to him where we go from here."

I nodded and asked, "What did you do to Hansen back there in the restroom?"

"I told him I would drown him in his own piss if he didn't tell me the truth."

"Did he?"

"No, he won't admit to anything. But he doesn't have to anymore. If I can't believe him, nobody will. We all cut corners sometimes, and I don't expect all the evidence my cops bring in to be neat and pure, but this is too much."

We went inside and took the jail elevator back up to Judge Choy's court. The room was completely empty, not even a bailiff in attendance, and we both realized that it was still more than an hour before two o'clock. Casey told me to wait there while he left to find Lambert. I walked over and peered through the tiny window of the front door. A few people were lined up in the hallway, but I did not see Jennifer or Ralph's mother and sister. I wandered around the room for several minutes, my thoughts racing, until I heard the front doors open.

A deputy sheriff came in and said, "Mr. Armstrong, the District Attorney's office asked me to send you upstairs."

I followed him into the hallway, thanked him, and took the elevator to the third floor. Casey was waiting for me in the lobby. He led me past the receptionist and down the long corridor until we came to a large office and yet another receptionist, who opened the door and told us to go right in.

It was an even larger office than I had expected. In addition to the District Attorney's own desk, it contained a long conference table, several leather chairs, two couches, and an eight-foot grandfather clock. Floor-to-ceiling shelves filled with law books lined three walls, and a thick carpet covered the floor.

Lambert rose to greet us and introduced me to William Gollin, the District Attorney, who remained seated. We shook hands and I took a chair facing his desk.

"Inspector Casey has just told us some very disturbing things about the Rodriguez case, Mr. Armstrong. I understand you're aware of them. What do you propose we do?"

"Dismiss the indictment, " I said without hesitation.

Gollin leaned forward and said, "I don't think the judge will go that far. After all, even if the detective twisted some facts around, there's still a lot of evidence against Rodriguez. We know he's been riding around in that van for over a year posing as a maintenance man. God knows what he's been up to, but we found the Horn girl's panties in the van, and he has no alibi for that murder or any of the others. And we can connect him to all the victims through the Rape Bureau. I think we're all after the same thing here, Mr. Armstrong. No one

128

wants to see a miscarriage of justice, but none of us wants to turn loose a sex maniac, either."

"Mr. Gollin, Rodriguez has never been convicted of any crime, sex or otherwise," I argued.

"Come now, Mr. Armstrong, we all know he raped that girl. We can talk straight here."

He paused to look up at the ceiling, then made his offer.

"I'll go this far. We'll recommend dismissal of the indictment if you'll get Rodriguez to volunteer for confinement as a Mentally Abnormal Sex Offender. They'll treat him up at Vacaville as a patient, not as a convict, and he'll be free to go when he's cured."

I did not even consider accepting the suggestion. I knew that Ralph Rodriguez looked to me as his counsel for one thing—freedom—and did not care what Gollin or I or anybody else thought was best for him and society.

"I'm sorry, Mr. Gollin, but I have to protect my client's interests, and I think any judge will throw out the charges. There was no probable cause for the arrest. If Hansen had really found Rodriguez at the scene of the crime, he would have had reason to question him. But he simply went off looking for him on a hunch. Therefore he did not have cause, and all the evidence he discovered is inadmissible, including the confession."

Gollin glared at me across his desk, punching his finger for emphasis.

"You listen to me, mister. I don't give a damn about your technicalities. All I care about is guilt or innocence. If he killed those girls, he's going to pay, no matter what you do."

I remained as calm as I could. "We're not talking

about mere technicalities, sir. The arresting officer is lying. He's already perjured himself in court this morning. Inspector Casey knows it and I know it. I can understand your position, but I hope you understand mine. I'm not going to let my client be convicted on false testimony. If you'll agree to a dismissal, I assure you I'll say nothing to the press or anyone else about the reasons, and I'm sure I can get Rodriguez not to press a lawsuit against Hansen and the city."

No one else spoke for a moment, and the only sound in the room was the ticking of the large clock until Gollin stood up behind his desk.

"All right, Mr. Armstrong, but I promise you, here and now, this is not the end of it. We'll continue investigating, and if I'm convinced Rodriguez is the killer, I'll put him in the gas chamber if it's the last thing I ever do. In the meantime, I wouldn't even jaywalk if I were in his shoes." He turned to Lambert. "Go on back to court. I'll call Choy and tell him what we're doing."

Casey, Lambert and I shared the same elevator, but none of us spoke. Even though I knew that in a few minutes I would succeed in having my client exonerated, I did not feel victorious. I had won a battle with the state, but I could wish my client had been a little cleaner, the state a little dirtier. As it was, I felt vaguely unsatisfied, not at all sure that it had actually ended.

The spectators were already back in the courtroom, and I smiled at Jennifer and the Rodriguez women as I passed their aisle.

When Ralph was brought back to the table, I said, "You're going home," but Judge Choy returned to the bench, preventing an explanation.

The entire process happened so quickly that it was anticlimactic. Nobody in the courtroom except the judge and me and Lambert knew what was going on. Judge Choy asked me if I had a motion, which I made, and when Lambert offered no objection, the judge ordered the indictment dismissed. After rapping his gavel, he disappeared into his chambers. The decision left the audience momentarily stunned, but soon the courtroom was in an uproar of surprise and questioning.

Ralph's wife and mother and Jennifer rushed past the railing, and I ushered them into the conference room behind the court, closing the door against the advancing reporters.

I tried to explain exactly what had taken place, but all that Ralph wanted to hear was that he had been released. He held his mother in his arms while his wife sat by his side and they all wept, commiserating with one another in Spanish. I knew enough of the language to recognize what "hijo" and "madre" meant and realized finally, if not for the first time, the intense relationship Ralph had with his mother, almost to the exclusion of his wife.

"There's just one thing I want you to know before I go," I said to all of them. "Ralph may be charged with these same crimes again. The case was dropped because of the way the police arrested him, but if they get some new evidence, they'll try again. Under the circumstances, I really don't think they will, but I wanted to tell you just in case."

There seemed to be nothing more to say, so Jennifer and I braced ourselves and went out into the swarm of reporters. Despite the gratitude I had seen in the tear-stained faces of my client and his family, I would be known to most people for some time as the lawyer who got the Bay Ripper off on a technicality.

12

News coverage was relentless after the dismissal. Since there had been no more murders of the Bay Ripper type in the area, it was generally assumed that Ralph Rodriguez had gotten away with the "crime of the century," and he and his family moved to San Diego to escape the publicity. Although I was fearful that each new day might bring renewed charges, my letters to Ralph told him that everything would be all right and encouraged him to start a new life.

I had received calls from several prospective clients, but my time was taken up in meetings with Burger involving the slander litigation against Mackay and the television station, and I had not yet accepted a new case. Also, Jennifer and I had been trying to relax, spending a lot of evenings alone and catching up on movies.

On Friday morning I had an appointment to defend one of our friends in a traffic case. Jennifer and I planned to leave for a weekend in Bodega Bay as soon as I was finished. I kissed her warm neck before I left, nuzzling her half-awake, reminding her that we wanted to get an early start.

The traffic court hearing was successful. I talked with the prosecutor for a few moments and worked out an agreement for my friend to plead guilty to a less serious offense—speeding—for which he would receive only a small fine. We went through the motions quickly in front of the judge. My friend was so pleased that when we were outside, on the steps of the building, he insisted I accept a twenty-dollar bill for my trouble. I had had every intention of performing my services as a personal favor, but I finally accepted the money. It was the first fee I had ever earned as a lawyer, and I cherished it.

I returned to the apartment in Sausalito to find Jennifer packed and ready for our weekend trip. We were both excited by the prospect of the long, leisurely drive up the coast and of seeing Abe again. On the way out of town we stopped long enough for me to spend my entire morning's earnings on one bottle of twenty-five-year-old scotch.

When we got to Bodega Bay it was late afternoon, but there was still enough sun left to spend an hour or so on the deck. Abe joined us, closing the garage as soon as we arrived, and we presented him with the scotch. It was his favorite brand, and he beamed with pleasure as he poured each of us some of the rare liquid.

After we had finished our first drink, Abe placed a ten-gallon can of water on his outdoor grill and lighted a fire beneath it. When the water came to a boil, he tossed in seaweed, potatoes, corn on the cob, a dozen clams, and three live crabs.

"There," he announced, putting a lid on the can. "Dinner will be ready shortly, but we still have time for another drink."

We savored the scotch and one another's company and watched the fishing boats return to port as the setting sun gradually lowered itself onto the distant horizon. Our calm was interrupted by the ringing of the telephone, and Abe got up to answer it. Jennifer and I heard him invite the caller to stop by, even offering to throw another crab into the pot. Eventually Abe returned to the deck to tell us he had been talking with Inspector Casey.

"He wanted to know if you were here, David. He's coming by to talk with you."

"About Rodriguez?" I wondered.

Abe shook his head. "He didn't say. He got this number from your answering service, and since he was already in Santa Rosa he said he might as well see you here."

"What's he doing in Santa Rosa?"

"I don't know, but he'll be here soon, so let's eat."

Abe and I grasped the can by its handles and emptied the entire contents onto the wooden picnic table. What remained after the hot water had drained through the slats and off the deck was our feast. The combination of fresh seafood and vegetables produced a fantastic aroma and taste, but I ate without my usual enthusiasm. Casey's impending visit, and the bad news I expected he was bringing for Ralph, dominated my thoughts.

We had finished our dinner and had retreated inside from the cool night air when Casey arrived. He looked grim, and there was a moment of awkward formality before he accepted Jennifer's offer to join us for coffee.

"I appreciate your letting me barge in on you like this," Casey said as we settled around the kitchen table. "I mainly came to talk to Mr. Armstrong, but now that we're all together, I'd like to thank you in person, Mr. Davidson."

"Thank me?" Abe asked.

"Yes, sir, for the phone call. It seemed like a small thing at the time, but it started me on the right track."

Abe responded to mine and Jennifer's bewildered expressions. "It was just a hunch. I didn't tell you because it would have distracted David from the trial."

Casey said, "I'm sorry, Mr. Davidson. I thought they knew or I wouldn't have . . ."

Abe waved his hand. "No, it's all right, Inspector."

Jennifer and I were still baffled, and Abe explained, "I was playing amateur detective. After you and I visited Doctor Paley in her home that day, David, I called the Inspector and told him about the TV. She had said she was unaware of the Bay Ripper murders because she never read newspapers, yet the television was on all the time. Since she must have seen at least one of the countless news reports or bulletins, I began to wonder."

Casey nodded and added, "Because of that, I thought back to the night that Hansen volunteered to take Wendy Horn to her aunt's house. The Assistant D.A., Pell, Doctor Paley and I were all standing outside the courtroom then. Paley is the only one of us who can't prove where she was that night. Her alibi is that she spent the evening at home with her father. That's when I thought I should start doing some checking on Paley, try to find out more about her."

136

Casey paused to loosen his tie, then lit a cigarette and sipped some coffee. He looked tired.

"I've spent the past several days in Santa Rosa," he continued, "and I've got a pretty complete picture now. Doctor Paley, the old man, was the most prominent physician in town. For years he was the only one. He utilized part of his house as an office and clinic, and his oldest daughter, Charlotte, was constantly in his company. Everyone who remembers Charlotte Paley says they never thought she would be anything but a doctor. All through school she had few friends or outside interests; she spent all of her free time in her father's office. She had a younger sister who was exactly the opposite—outgoing and popular with boys and girls her own age. Her sister apparently identified more with the mother, who was fourteen years younger than the father and was by all accounts a stunningly beautiful woman. She and the younger daughter totally disappeared one day, about two years before Doctor Paley entered UC Berkeley. Since most of Mrs. Paley's clothing and personal belongings were also missing, as well as the girl's, the police surmised that she had taken her favorite child and run away in the night, perhaps even with another man. Some of the oldtimers in the Santa Rosa police department remember that there was some talk of foul play, but nothing ever came of it. Because Doctor Paley was such a respected figure in the community—he was even the coroner at the time— there was never any real suspicion that he or his older daughter had any involvement in the disappearance. In any event, the mother and the younger daughter were never heard from again, and when Doctor Paley enrolled in college her father sold his practice to a young physician and moved to San Francisco with her."

Casey's cigarette had burned down to the filter, and he dropped it into an ashtray.

"That was the whole story," he said, "until yesterday. I got a search warrant for the house and grounds, and we found what I expected. The luggage and clothes first, and then the bodies. They were fairly well decomposed, but the autopsy positively identified them as the mother and sister. The cause of death was, of course, multiple stab wounds. They had both been ripped apart."

We were all silent for a time. Finally I asked Casey, "Have you charged Paley with the Bay Ripper murders?"

"No, I haven't. And I'm not sure if I'll ever be able to."

"Knowing what you know, you're going to let her run loose?"

"Of course not. We'll get a conviction for the Santa Rosa killings, but we don't have enough evidence yet to pin the Ripper murders on her."

"You've got the bodies of her mother and sister," I argued, "cut up like the later victims, and you've got the fact that out of all the people who knew Wendy Horn's whereabouts the night she was murdered, only Doctor Paley has no alibi."

"I know, I know. It looks like a neat package. We can show opportunity, also. Not only did she know all the victims, she had previously examined each of them, usually in their homes. Which explains how she was able to get to the girls in the midst of all the fear and publicity. She would have been admitted without question as a woman and a doctor they already knew. But we

138

need more than that. After the embarrassment of the
Rodriguez dismissal, the D.A. would never go into
court without direct evidence linking her to those murders. And where's the motive? Why would a woman do
those things to other women?"

He paused for some scotch, then continued: "You
know, between the Zodiac and the Ripper, somebody's
been leaving young girls' bodies lying around this city
for years. I've often tried to imagine what kind of person
the killer was and what I would do when I caught the
weird, screwed-up son-of-a-bitch. I had a mental picture of him. He had a fat face and little pig eyes, and I
could imagine myself choking him until his eyes popped
out or until he begged for mercy. But now that I've
finally solved the case, I end up with a woman. A
damned woman." He shook his head. "I can't figure it."

"You must have seen your share of female murderers," Abe said.

"Yes, sir, plenty of them. But not mass murderers.
The sequential, premeditated woman killer is very rare.
And brutal knife attacks on other women are rarer still."

Abe thought a moment before replying. "I'm not an
expert on murder, Inspector, but from my perspective
there are aggressive personalities in both sexes, and it
would seem to me that an aggressive woman could kill
just as ruthlessly as an aggressive man. I can't see where
femininity and violence are incompatible. I'm sure
you're not saying that women murderers are all little old
ladies who kill only with poison."

"Of course not. We had a string of lover's lane shoot-
ings several years ago, and the killer turned out to be a
teen-aged girl from Oakland. She just rode around in a
pickup with a high-powered rifle hunting people like

they were animals. I don't say it doesn't happen. It's just rare. But who knows? The latest theory now is that even Jack the Ripper was a woman, a Jane the Ripper. I learned something a long time ago about murder investigations. The only facts you eliminate are the untrue and the impossible. Whatever remains, however improbable, must be the truth."

I poured some more scotch into our glasses as I said, "Speaking of the impossible, how do you explain the semen in Wendy Horn's body?"

"Hansen," Casey said. "They had intercourse shortly before she was killed."

I nodded, my last doubts dispelled. "Well, I hope you're able to prove Paley's guilt. If it comes out that she's the Bay Ripper, my client will be completely off the hook."

"I know, Mr. Armstrong. That's exactly why I came here tonight. I need your help. I'd like you to come along when I question Doctor Paley's father."

"I'm not sure I understand what you mean."

"I'm not sure I know myself, Mr. Armstrong. All I know is that we've had Paley in custody since yesterday and she's not about to talk. All we have left is her father. He's still in the house with a nurse until we decide what to do with him. I'm going there tomorrow morning to interrogate him, but there's really nothing I can do or say to persuade him to help us. He's a sick old man already facing death, so threats of punishment or confinement are not going to mean anything to him. You have a right to go there with me, as an officer of the court, representing your client. I have no idea how he might react to your presence, but at least you can appeal to him from a different perspective. You're not a policeman and you're trying to help clear Rodriguez. I doubt if it'll work, but I think it's the only hope we've got. What do you say?"

I agreed, and we arranged to meet at the house on Bush Street at nine the next morning.

There seemed to be nothing more to say, and after draining the last of his drink from his glass Casey stood up and offered Abe his hand and his thanks. He thanked Jennifer also, for her hospitality, and then we all escorted him outside to his car.

We said our final good-bys and watched his car disappear down the ocean highway before deciding to take a walk. I went back inside for our coats, and then Abe, Jennifer and I strolled along the water's edge. We were silent with our individual thoughts, and it was not until we were on our way back to the house that Jennifer broke the conversational lull.

"Inspector Casey has convinced me," she said, "even if he can't prove it in court. She did it. But I don't understand why. Why would she kill all those girls who had absolutely nothing to do with her and nothing to do with one another? It just doesn't make sense."

"It never will if you look to the external circumstances for an explanation," Abe said. "The answer lies within Doctor Paley's unconscious. That's the reason people always say that certain murderers seemed normal and well adjusted. The emotions that caused them to kill were repressed."

Jennifer picked up a rock and flung it into the dark waters. "I know that's how you feel, but I don't give a damn about her or her problems. All I can think about is what she did to those girls, and I hope they put her in the gas chamber."

141

"You have a perfect right to that feeling, Jennifer. My initial reaction is the same, but if we kill her, all it will do is satisfy our urge for revenge. If we successfully analyze her behavior, we will not only learn more about her, we will learn more about ourselves."

"How are you going to analyze her if she won't talk?"

"You're right. It's probably not possible. But we already know enough to get some idea of her personality. Based on what Inspector Casey told us he had found out, and from our own knowledge that she has lived with her father, exclusive of all other men, for all of her adult life, it is a reasonable supposition that she was involved in an incestuous relationship. Whether or not they physically consummated their pact is not so important—it was an incestuous affair nevertheless. The breaking of that taboo alone was almost certainly enough to prevent her from leading a healthy life, but she added to it an even more horrible taboo, matricide. Once she and her father decided to share that awful secret and live together in total isolation, both of them were ruined forever. We may never know exactly what caused Doctor Paley to kill those girls, but in light of what we do know, it is no mystery that she would do something terrible. She actually removed the sexual organs from those girls' bodies. When you think that someone like that, with that kind of conflict regarding femininity, was placed in charge of examining and treating rape victims . . . it was like letting a panther loose on a sheep farm."

Abe shuddered, whether from the cold or from the impact of his own words, and Jennifer and I hugged him between us as we walked back to the house.

142

13

Jennifer and I had driven back to Sausalito late Friday evening, so I left her sleeping in our apartment, which was already filling with morning sunlight, and drove up the hill into the fog that almost totally obscured the Golden Gate Bridge and the city beyond.

It was only eight-thirty, so I drove slower than the traffic around me on 19th Avenue, but I was still a few minutes early when I arrived in front of Paley's house on Bush Street. The street was empty and quiet except for a kid playing on a skateboard near the corner, and I waited until Casey and another man drove up in an unmarked police car. The other man was carrying a small black case, and Casey introduced him to me as a court reporter.

We walked up the steps to the house. A middle-aged

143

black woman answered the door. Her white uniform contrasted so sharply with her skin and the dark hallway that she appeared almost luminous.

When Casey showed her his badge, she escorted us into the living room, where the old man lay sleeping in his bed. The TV set was on, but we could not hear the sound, since the audio was connected to an ear plug. The nurse turned off the set, removed the plug from the man's ear and gently shook him awake.

He opened his eyes quickly, the only movement he made, and we could tell from the expression on his face that he knew why we were there.

"Are you taking me away?" he asked. "Where are you taking me?" The voice seemed surprisingly strong, emanating from the wrinkled and broken face.

Casey started to reply, but the nurse said, "You don't have to shout, Inspector. He's not that hard of hearing."

"All right," Casey said. In a voice only slightly louder than normal he identified himself and the reporter to the old man, then pointed to me and added, "And this is Mr. Armstrong. He's a private attorney representing his client who is involved in this case. Now, Doctor Paley, I understand that your rights were read to you when they arrested your daughter. Is that correct? Do you have any objection to talking with us?"

The reporter had already set up his little table and machine and was recording Casey's question.

"Talk?" the old man replied, shaking his white head. "I haven't talked to anybody but Charlotte for years. I don't see why I should change now."

"Do you really understand why we're here, sir?" Casey asked patiently.

The old man's eyes flashed as he glared directly at Casey. "Don't treat me like that, Mister Inspector. I know you've found the bodies, but I've lived a whole life with that knowledge. You can't scare me with it now. And I don't care." He moved for the first time, slightly forward. "Do you hear? I don't care. I saved thousands of lives in my time. Literally thousands. That balances off two deaths." He slumped back against his pillow and added, "Besides, it was an accident. She really didn't mean to do it."

Casey did not conceal his disgust as he said, "Those two deaths you refer to were your wife and your daughter, Doctor. And whether she meant to or not, your daughter hacked them to pieces."

"No," the old doctor argued. "It was an accident. Charlotte may have had a violent streak when she was young, but I cured her of that. I caught her once imitating my autopsies, but the poor cat wasn't dead yet. I put the thing out of its misery and explained to Charlotte that if she wanted to be a doctor like me, she would have to learn to ease pain, not cause it. And she did. She became a wonderful doctor."

"What about the deaths?" Casey prodded. "What caused the 'accident'?"

"Jealousy. Charlotte and I were always very close, and her mother was jealous. Plain and simple. And when Charlotte got older and her body began to develop, it became worse. Charlotte often had nightmares, and I would wake up in the morning to find her in bed with me. The meaning has not escaped me. After all, I am a doctor. But there was absolutely nothing like that between us. I would never . . ."

His voice trailed off as his eyes filled with tears.

". . . her mother came into the bedroom that morning and saw us, saw Charlotte sleeping there in her night-gown . . . and she began beating her. With her fists. I tried to stop her, but she was like a madwoman. I thought she was going to kill Charlotte. But Charlotte protected herself. My straight razor was lying on the dresser near the bed and she grabbed it. It happened so fast, there was nothing I could do. My younger daughter heard her mother's screams and came in to protect her, but Charlotte was in a frenzy and killed her too. The blood was everywhere, and it took us hours to clean up the room. We even had to move the bed to conceal the largest stain. Then we buried them, and we've never spoken of it since."

His eyes were literally gushing tears now, but he was not sobbing; his voice was not broken. "What could I do? It was clearly an accident, but I knew no one would understand. I couldn't let you take my daughter away for something she didn't mean to do."

I knew then that he had told us all he was going to tell us, but Casey indicated with a nod that it was my turn, so I tried anyway.

"Sir, as Inspector Casey told you," I began, "I represent a man who has been accused of the Bay Ripper murders. Do you know about those killings?"

He nodded almost imperceptibly and I continued: "The police have reason to believe that your daughter may be responsible for those crimes also. I know how you must feel now, but if you know anything, it might help an innocent man. Your daughter is going to be convicted of the other murders anyway, so it won't be any worse for her. Is there anything you can tell us, Doctor Paley?"

It was not my best plea, but I felt empty inside and not up to the task.

The old man had been staring at the ceiling as I spoke and did not look at me as he said, "You weren't listening, were you? It was an accident. Charlotte never intended to hurt anyone, and she's spent the rest of her life atoning for her mistake. How could you believe she would do these things after what I've told you?" The nurse offered him a tissue, and when he did not respond she wiped some of the tears off his face.

Casey seemed to want me to continue, but I stood up and walked out into the hallway. I heard Casey give some instructions to the nurse, and then he and the reporter followed me outside.

"I'm sorry, Inspector," I said. "I know I should have pressed harder, but I couldn't wait to get out of there."

"I understand, but he wasn't going to tell us any more anyway. I doubt if he knows anything."

We walked toward our cars and I said good-by to the reporter. Casey and I looked at each other. "So where does this leave us?" I asked.

"Where we were before. All I can do is prosecute her for killing her mother and sister, even though *I* know she's the Ripper and *you* know she's the Ripper. The public will never know the truth, but at least she'll be off the street."

"Which means Ralph Rodriguez will have to go through the rest of his life with people thinking he's a mass murderer."

"That doesn't bother me a whole hell of a lot, Armstrong. He deserves some trouble for what he did. And as long as this rap's hanging over his head, he'll think twice before even going near another girl. That and the fact that we're putting Paley away anyway means there'll be a little justice, after all. That's what we all want, isn't it?"

"For others, it is," I said. "When it comes to ourselves, I'm sure we would prefer mercy."

"Yeah, I suppose," Casey admitted reluctantly, then gave me his hand. "Well, good-by, Armstrong. I'm sure I'll see you around. And thanks for coming here today, even though it didn't work out as well as we hoped."

"You're welcome," I said, shaking his hand. "By the way, speaking of justice, whatever happened with Inspector Hansen?"

"Not much. He's still facing a departmental hearing, but cops are civil servants, and it's almost impossible to fire them. He's still got to face me, though. I reassigned him to burglary, and as long as I'm Chief of Inspectors he'll have a rough time."

"Well, give him my regards," I said, and Casey grinned as he got into the car with the reporter and drove away.

When I got back to the Golden Gate, it was still enveloped in great gray swirls of fog. I crossed the bridge and took the first exit, continuing down the hill road in fog until I broke out near the bottom. The little bay town was just as I had left it earlier in the morning, enjoying, as always, a cloudless day. Jennifer and I had often discussed the phenomenon. We did not know whether it was because of the protection of the surrounding mountains or the effect of the sea-level elevation—or a combination of the two—but Sausalito seemed always to provide us sunlight in the midst of fog, and we considered it our Shangri-La.

The newspapers reported the arrests of Doctor Paley

and her father but did not connect them to the Bay Ripper murders. And several weeks later it was an nounced that the Sonoma County District Attorney had accepted a guilty plea with the understanding that both of the Paleys would be committed to a state hospital, presumably for the rest of their lives.

As a proper ending to the case, Benjamin Burger telephoned to tell me that Carolyn Mackay and her station were willing to settle out of court for thirty thousand dollars. Burger reminded me that we would be splitting the money down the middle and seemed to want to hold out for more, but I instructed him to make the deal.

Fifteen thousand would enable me to continue practicing the kind of criminal law I wanted to for a while, and it was a lot more than I thought my reputation was worth to begin with.